LIGHTNING LOU

LIGHTNING LOU

LORI WEBER

DCB

**Canada Council
for the Arts** **Conseil des Arts
du Canada** 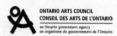 ONTARIO ARTS COUNCIL
CONSEIL DES ARTS DE L'ONTARIO
an Ontario government agency
un organisme du gouvernement de l'Ontario

 Canadian   Patrimoine
Heritage   canadien   Canadä

The publisher gratefully acknowledges the support of the Canada Council for the
Arts and the Ontario Arts Council for its publishing program. We acknowledge
the financial support of the Government of Canada through the Canada Book
Fund (CBF) for our publishing activities, and the Government of Ontario through
the Ontario Media Development Corporation, an agency of the Ontario Ministry
of Culture, and the Ontario Book Publishing Tax Credit Program.

LIBRARY AND ARCHIVES CANADA CATALOGUING IN PUBLICATION

Weber, Lori, 1959–, author
Lightning Lou / Lori Weber.

Issued in print and electronic formats.
ISBN 978-1-77086-462-7 (paperback). — ISBN 978-1-77086-463-4 (html)

I. Title.

PS8645.E24L53 2016   JC813'.6   C2015-907525-4
                                        C2015-907526-2

Cover art and design: Nick Craine
Interior text design: Tannice Goddard, Soul Oasis Networking
Printer: Friesens

Printed and bound in Canada.

 MIX
Paper from
responsible sources
FSC   FSC® C016245
www.fsc.org

The interior of this book is printed on 100% post-consumer waste recycled paper.

DANCING CAT BOOKS
an imprint of Cormorant Books Inc.
10 ST. MARY STREET, SUITE 615, TORONTO, ONTARIO, M4Y 1P9
www.cormorantbooks.com

For Simon and Michael, and Liam and Casey,
and all young people with big dreams everywhere.

One

Lou pulled the long black skirt over the thick wool stockings Maman had knit in the summer while sitting out on the porch under the maple tree. There was no way to go out on the ice without those stockings. Not today, and not anytime soon. By mid-November, the temperature in this part of the world was well below zero. Lou thought it was paradise. Not the kind of paradise the Bible talked about, a place called Eden, which was full of greenery and sand. This was a northern paradise made of snow and ice. The greatest paradise on earth!

Lou grabbed the bright red tuque Maman had also knit and pulled it on. "Keep your ears covered," Maman always warned. "Or you'll get frostbite." That was especially true now, when there were no leaves on the trees to cut the wind that howled along the lake, blowing straight down from Maniwaki.

Lou shifted and squirmed under the skirt, trying to get comfortable. The ice was crackling, just beyond the shed, and Lou could hear the squealing of girls who were already out there, warming up.

"Lou Lou. Lou Lou," Maman called.

Oh no! Why did Maman always call at the wrong time? It would be hard to cut around her and leave the house without being seen.

But Lou had to win that bet with Francine. The only way out would be to sneak past the kitchen and run. Maybe, with any luck, Maman would be distracted by Mouffle. That cat was terribly fond of Maman's baking and would wrap himself around her ankles in the hopes of a fallen crumb. Maman never moved when Mouffle was at her feet for fear of stepping on the animal's tail.

Lou tiptoed down the stairs, coat already on, and made a run for it, leaping over Mouffle, who was curled up on the braided rug in front of the door.

The coach was already on the ice, ordering the girls to skate in a wide circle, round and round, as he watched. The coach had come for one day only to recruit players for his team in the girls' hockey league, and he would not like that Lou was late. It was bad enough that he'd come to a small town that was practically in the middle of nowhere; a latecomer was not going to impress him. The poster at the train station had said that the coach was not from Quebec. He was from Ontario, but he had a French name, Étienne Robichaud, and he spoke French, which was lucky since Lou didn't speak much English. None of the kids in town did, except the son and daughter of the man who owned the sawmill where Papa worked.

Still, you didn't need language to play hockey. You could be deaf or from another planet and still play, as long as you could skate and handle the puck on the end of your stick.

Head down, Lou pushed into the circle of girls. Francine and Paulette looked as though an alien had just fallen onto the ice from the sky. They screwed up their eyebrows and shouted, "Hey, don't be so pushy."

Lou turned to Francine and smiled. It was fun to watch her face turn from angry to surprised. Her eyes grew big and round, and her mouth opened wide. But before she could speak, Lou skated off.

Today was not the day to hold back. No siree. Lou did two gentle rounds to warm up, then decided it was time to let loose. Monsieur Robichaud held a clipboard in his hands and he was taking notes. That meant the poster hadn't lied. This man really was here to find the best female hockey player, one that could rival Albertine Lapensée, the Miracle Maid from Cornwall. The poster said that Albertine had scored eighty percent of her team's goals last year. Not only that, it also said that she was one of the best hockey players ever born, male or female.

"I should try out," Francine had said when she saw the poster on their way home from school.

"Yeah, you should," Lou had responded. "And so should I."

"You? You wouldn't dare," said Francine.

"Watch me," said Lou. And now here they were, skating for this big shot coach from Ontario.

The trick to skating fast was in the thighs. They were the powerhouse for the legs, the same way the wild water in the stream was the powerhouse for the sawmill on the other side of the hill, hidden from view. Lou pumped and pumped and was soon skating circles around the rest of the girls, doing two laps for every one of theirs. The girls could stick out their tongues and complain all they wanted. One even stuck out her foot — no problem. Lou just jumped over it and kept on flying, pretending it was an opponent's stick.

All that mattered now was the way Monsieur Robichaud's eyes were locked onto Lou. Locked fast, like they were held there by a magnet. He was scribbling away on his pad. And he was smiling under his huge moustache — smiling the way Papa smiled when he heard that his favorite player, Edouard "Newsy" Lalonde of the Montreal Canadiens, had scored a goal. When the daily paper came to town on the train from Montreal, the station master, Monsieur Geoffrion, was always the first to know the latest scores. If he had time he'd walk down to the mill, where most of the men in town worked, and spread the news, good or bad. Lou could tell if the Canadiens had won by Papa's mood when he walked through the door: bright if they had, dark if they hadn't.

Monsieur Robichaud blew his whistle and pulled a stopwatch out of his pocket. Then he threw several pucks onto the ice. "Get your sticks, girls," he called out. "I want you to carry the puck all the way around the lake as fast as you can." Not all the girls had sticks, but Lou and Francine were lucky — they had their older brothers' hand-me-downs. Other girls pushed the pucks with their skates, some with branches torn from trees.

Lou zoomed around the ice, never once losing the puck, even when Francine tried poking it away. There was no way this Albertine Lapensée could skate any faster. "Great time," Monsieur Robichaud called out when Lou returned to where the coach was standing.

Francine came in a close second. She was beaming, her cheeks rosy red under her tuque. "You too," said the coach. "Not too bad." Francine turned and stuck her tongue out at Lou.

"That's it, girls," the coach called out when all the girls had returned. "Thanks so much for coming out today. You can all go home, except for you two." He pointed to Lou and Francine. "I'm interested in both of you," he said. "What are your names?"

"I'm Francine and this is Lou —"

"Lou Lou, monsieur," said Lou quickly, holding out a hand, showing a sense of manners that would make Maman proud. Maman would also approve of the pet name, Lou Lou. Only Maman used it. Papa never did. He did not approve.

"Well, Francine and Lou Lou, how would you like to play on a real team?"

"We'd love it, wouldn't we, Francine?"

"Well, sure, but how and where?"

"The team is going to be big. We're in Montreal, so you'd have to leave home. We're called the Bakers. The owner, Monsieur Oliver, is a great businessman. He owns the biggest bakery in the city, maybe even the country, and he's very wealthy. Each player receives ten dollars per month. You'd board at his sister's house. She'd chaperone you too, of course."

Francine was already shaking her head. "There's no way for me," she said. "My parents wouldn't agree. My mother needs me at home. I have three younger siblings, and I'm the eldest girl left. My older sisters are all married."

"It's a shame," said the coach. "You have talent. Not quite at Lapensée's level yet. But with time, who knows? Are you sure?"

"Yes, I am." Lou watched Francine's eyes fill with tears. It must have been hard for her to say no. Francine loved hockey every bit as much as Lou did. Everyone in town knew that. They'd been playing since they were little, spending every spare minute out on the ice — before school, after school, and all weekend long, with nothing to stop them but the occasional blast of freezing rain. Or their parents, calling them in to do more chores. And the ten dollars a month would go a long way toward helping Francine's family too. Like Lou's, they didn't have a lot of money. No one in their small town did, except the man who owned the sawmill.

"And Lou Lou can't either, because —"

"Oh yes, I can," Lou jumped in. "You don't need to answer for me."

"But this isn't fair," said Francine, waving her stick.

"Now, now, my dear," said the coach. "Sportsmanship is the name of the game, especially for girls."

Francine was steaming. Lou imagined her raven hair curling under her tuque. "Fine," she said. "You'll see."

The coach turned to Lou. "Well, my dear, I guess that leaves you."

Francine turned for home. Her shoulders were stooped, and she walked slowly, as though she wanted to take forever to get there. Lou couldn't let her go off like that. He ran after her.

"Francine, don't be mad," he whispered, pulling on her arm.

"You know you can't do this, Lou," she said.

"Why not?"

"Because, Lou. In case you forgot, you're a boy!"

Two

ou had barely pulled off the long black skirt when
Maman burst into the room. "There you are," she
said, sitting on the edge of Lou's bed. "Didn't you hear
me call you before?"

"Yes, Maman, but I was busy."

"Busy? Too busy for your old maman? And too busy
for a piece of molasses bread? Are you sick?"

Lou laughed and watched Maman pull a thick slab of
buttered bread, folded in half, out of her apron pocket.
Just in time! There was nothing like skating to work up
a fierce appetite. Lou bit in. "It's so good, Maman. The
best."

Lou thought Maman would be pleased, but instead
she looked down and sighed. She reached into her large
apron pocket and pulled out a piece of paper.

Oh no, don't let it be from school, Lou thought. It was
just so hard to concentrate once the ice hardened and
all Lou could think about was playing hockey. What

could it matter where China was — did they even play hockey there? — or how many provinces were in Canada, or how long it would take to travel one thousand miles going sixty miles an hour. Lou had no intention of ever going that far, not unless it was to play hockey. Besides, no one went to school past the age of fourteen, and Lou would be there in two years.

"Maman, I —," Lou started to explain.

"It's from Georges, Lou Lou. Your brother. He's in Belgium — so far away. Can you believe it? He wrote to me and Papa, and to you too. Come sit by me and help me read it."

Lou's eyes lit up. A letter from Georges, finally. He had shipped out six months ago with the rest of the 22nd Regiment, along with his two best friends from town. They'd signed up in the spring, infuriating their families. Papa had said there was no need. Conscription was just a rumor, in spite of that new law. Prime Minister Borden would never have the nerve to enforce it. Besides, didn't Georges know that French Canadians were treated like dirt in the army?

"Not in the *vingt-deuxième*, Papa," Georges had tried to explain. "It's ours, and I want to be part of it."

They hadn't heard a word from Georges since he left. Oh, the things he must be seeing. Now Lou wished that big old map from school was close by so they could see where Belgium was. It was somewhere in Europe, for sure, but where exactly?

"Okay, Maman. Move over." Lou took the paper and started to read.

Chers Maman, Papa, and Lou

I cannot write for long because it's very dark in this hole, and even though Steven, my new English friend, is holding matches for me, I cannot see very well. Also, we mustn't let too much light travel up because the enemy will see us. But, Maman, I don't want you to worry about that. The enemy is not very close. In fact, the only enemy I've seen so far is the water that is always pooling under our feet. It's not cold enough to turn into ice, like at home.

So, Maman, I cannot tell you how much I appreciate all those socks you knit for me and stuffed into my bag. I gave Steven a pair because his mother doesn't know how to knit. Steven says she is good for nothing except looking pretty. I would never say such a thing about you, Maman. You are good for so many things and you are pretty too. Papa, please tell Maman that she is pretty for me, every day, until I come home. And you, Lou? I imagine you're out on the ice already, practicing your slap shot. Don't forget that you are not the star of this family. You're only keeping the ice warm (haha!) until I get back. You know my shot is harder and more precise than yours. Never forget that, little brother, never.

I have to go. Love to you all, Georges

P.S. They speak French here, can you imagine? I never knew.

Three

That night at supper, Lou knew he'd have to tell Maman and Papa about what had happened earlier, after the skate. But it wasn't going to be easy, especially with Papa. Lou could barely believe it himself. Had he actually said yes to playing hockey on a girls' team? The whole thing had started as a joke. He'd never meant to take it seriously, not until it turned into a real offer. But could he make Papa see it that way?

"Louis, pass the beans," said Papa. The skin on his hands was rough and nicked with cuts from the wood he had to pass between huge round blades at the sawmill. Georges had once suggested that he wear gloves, but Papa had said that would be more dangerous. "You need to be agile," he'd said. "You need to feel the wood beneath your skin. Sometimes it moves just an eighth of an inch to the right or left, which could be a disaster. With gloves on, I'd never know. And if I slice off my fingers, who will work and put food on our table?"

Lou lifted the pot of beans and passed it across to Papa. He breathed in deeply — it was now or never. "I made it onto a team today," he said quickly, shoveling a piece of meatloaf into his mouth to cover up his nerves.

"A team? What do you mean?" asked Papa. "Are you and your friends getting a little game together?"

"No, Papa. A team, a real team."

"But there are no more teams since your brother and his friends went off to Europe," said Papa, not trying to disguise his anger. "We'll be lucky if there's any hockey at all this time next year. Borden won't rest until every young man in Quebec is carrying a gun. One day you and your brother will learn. English Canadians don't even remember that French Canadians exist, until they need something from us."

Lou had heard the speech a hundred times before, from Papa and others, but it was getting worse now that talk of conscription was everywhere. Posters hung at the train station, calling men to action. One showed a mother and child lying dead on the ground with a nasty German soldier standing over them, his large teeth like a rabid wolf's. It said, "C'est le moment d'agir" — it is time to take action — and Lou agreed. He was proud of Georges. His brother had taken that message to heart.

Lou couldn't help feeling that it was time for him to take action too, but what kind of action could a twelve-year-old boy find in this sleepy little town? If he couldn't be a hero on the battlefield, he could at least try to be one on the ice. He'd be the boy to prove that poster wrong: there was no way Albertine Lapensée, or any other girl, could play hockey better than a boy.

"It's a new team, with a real coach, Monsieur Robichaud. He was here today, and he saw me skate."

"Oh yeah, Monsieur Geoffrion told us a stranger came to town on the ten-thirty. Are you saying he wants you to play on his team?"

"Yes," said Lou, smiling widely. "That is exactly what I'm saying." He didn't say anything more about it, and neither did Papa. That meant he hadn't seen the poster himself. Or else he had, but he couldn't read it. His parents had always told him that going to school to learn to read and write was a privilege, and at that exact moment he was glad they'd never had such a privilege.

"But where is this team, Lou Lou? And who else is on it?" asked Maman.

"I'll find out more on the weekend, when the coach comes back. I'll tell you then. Now, do you want me to read Georges's letter again?" Lou asked. Once he had reread the letter, they would all be thinking about Georges. But they were always thinking of Georges, who had filled the little house with so much laughter. Theirs was a small family, the smallest in town. Maman had not been able to have more kids after Lou, and in between her two sons she had lost three. Lou didn't know why. But she always said that she had the two best. Everyone loved Georges, who was always ready with a joke. And Lou had been born early, small and delicate as an angel.

He hated it when she reminded him of that. Angels did not play hockey. And he wasn't small and delicate anymore. He was average in height, but solid, like Georges had been at his age, even if Georges did like to call him "Petit Lou" to bug him.

Four

For the next few days, Lou did his homework and his chores without having to be told. That way his parents would leave him alone. He needed time to think. Sure, the tryout had started off as a joke between him and Francine, but once the coach had said he wanted him, Lou started to think about the whole thing differently. What if he could pull it off? What if he could get to Montreal, the biggest city in Canada, and play on a real team, in a real arena? It would be a dream come true. Well, almost. Dressing as a girl wasn't part of the dream, but if it meant playing in the same city as the Montreal Canadiens, the team that both Georges and Lou hoped to play for one day, it might be worth it. It wasn't like any boys' team coaches were knocking on his door to take him away.

But Lou had to figure out a plan before Monsieur Robichaud came back to talk to his parents, like he'd said he would.

"I've got three more towns to visit, Lou Lou, then I'll be back," Monsieur Robichaud had said. "I'll need to talk to your parents, of course, explain it all to them, especially given your age." He placed his hand on Lou's shoulder and squeezed gently. Lou hoped he didn't have too much muscle there. He knew himself, from squeezing Francine's shoulder once at church, that girls' shoulders were nothing but bone.

"No problem, monsieur," Lou had replied, tugging at his hair under his tuque to make it look longer. Thank God he'd let it grow, even though Papa was always after Maman to cut it. Papa didn't like it when Lou did anything that resembled what a girl would do. He hated it when Lou helped Maman roll dough, which he did from time to time. When Maman had finished filling the dough with brown sugar and butter, sometimes chopped-up pecans, she'd let him lick the spoon. Papa even refused to call him Lou Lou. It was Louis or nothing.

What would Papa do when Lou came down the stairs to meet Monsieur Robichaud in a skirt? Lou trembled just thinking about his reaction. Papa could ruin everything.

Lou decided he'd have to tell Maman first, so she could warn Papa. It was the only way. Except he'd leave out the part about ripping the long black skirt off Madame Doucette's washing line last week. She might not forgive that. And how would she hold a straight face when Madame Doucette came by on the third Saturday of the month for the knitting circle? Lou had watched the group of women, their needles clicking and clacking so fast they were just a blur as they gossiped and worried about the village boys who were already so far away and others who would be forced to join them in time, unless a miracle intervened. The pile of vests and socks they were knitting to send to them grew on the braided rug between them, as though the rug were spitting them up.

Lou found Maman in the kitchen, kneading bread.

"Ah, you've come to help?" she asked, pointing to two lumps of dough waiting for attention.

"No, Maman. I came to tell you something. You know that team I told you about?"

Maman nodded as she worked, her sleeves rolled up.

"Well, I left out one small detail."

Maman stopped kneading and scratched the tip of her nose, leaving a white dot of flour. "Well?"

Lou took a deep breath and felt his face flush. "It is a girls' team."

"A what?"

"You heard me, Maman. A girls' team. They're popular now."

"Yes, I know. Father Béliveau talked about them. Remember?" Lou did remember. The priest had told everyone that girls' hockey teams were sprouting up like mushrooms all across the country, taking over the men's rinks, with so many men away at war. Then Father Béliveau had said that there was no way he'd allow such a team to exist in Saint-Christophe. "It isn't natural," he'd said. "Girls sweating and ramming into each other. The only reason people go to watch them play is curiosity, the same way they go to see animals at the zoo. We will not allow our young women, our future wives and mothers, to become spectacles. We will not allow young women to harm the bodies that were put on earth for God's purpose, to bear children, many, many children."

"But, Lou Lou, I don't understand. How can you play on a girls' team?"

"By pretending to be a girl, Maman. How else?"

Maman stared at him wide-eyed and slapped her cheeks, leaving floured finger marks on her face. "Lou. I don't know what to say. How can you do that? And why would you want to?"

"Because, Maman, I want to play hockey in the big city. I want to try it, just once. Think of it as a joke. As my little joke. I'll just play a few games, then I'll come back."

Maman forgot the dough and threw her arms around Lou. "But, Lou Lou, we cannot lose you now. Not so soon after Georges."

"That's it, Maman? That's all you have to say about it?"

"I know what you're thinking, my son," she continued. "I should be screaming because you are turning yourself into a girl. But let me tell you, I would rather have Georges dressed as a girl but safe and sound in Quebec than dressed as a soldier and hiding in a hole with Germans shooting all around him."

Maman squeezed him closer to her big bosom, which always smelled of flour. She paused, then looked down at him tenderly. "But if this is what you really want, Lou Lou, I won't stop you."

He knew Maman would be on his side. She always was, like the time he had broken the church window, flicking a rock against the wall with his stick and missing.

"And I'll be making money, too, Maman," Lou added, pulling back. "Enough so that you can order your-self something nice from the Eaton's catalogue this Christmas."

"Oh, Lou. Wouldn't it be nice to use the catalogue for something other than kindling or the outhouse?"

"And Papa will like that too, won't he, Maman?"

"Papa! Oh, Lou, you leave your papa to me. He may think he makes the rules around here, but don't you worry. I have my ways. Papa won't stop you either. No son of mine will be held back from getting ahead, even if that son must become a daughter."

Five

The night before Monsieur Robichaud's visit, Lou couldn't sleep. He lay awake, worrying that the coach might have found out about him somewhere. He'd gone off up the rail line, toward Wakefield, to look for more girls, but what if he'd talked about Lou Lou to his host families along the way? What if he'd described him at dinner, over a plate of *paté chinois*? He could see the family, the maman and papa and all the kids shaking their heads and saying that in all the times they'd come to Saint-Christophe to watch their team play against the Castors, they had never noticed such a girl. Thank God Lou hadn't mentioned his brother, Georges. Everyone in the valley knew Georges, and they knew that Georges did not have a sister.

Monsieur Robichaud knew where to come because Lou had pointed out his house, white against white, through the trees. "That's where I live," he'd said, barely opening his mouth and keeping his voice to a whisper.

"The one with the red door." Father Béliveau hated that red door and had tried to talk Maman into painting it back to white. Papa had defended her, saying it was bad enough the priest stuck his nose into all their affairs. They should be allowed to control their own doors.

"You *are* a quiet one," the coach had said, laughing. "But you don't skate quiet. You're the fastest skater and puck handler I've seen yet. Almost as fast as the Miracle Maid."

Lou tossed and turned in the dark, thinking of the nickname he would one day have when he became a star in the National Hockey Association. Like Georges Vézina, who played goalie for the Canadiens. He was from Chicoutimi, on the other side of Quebec, so they called him the Chicoutimi Cucumber because of how cool he stayed under pressure. Puck after puck might whip toward him and he would just stand and turn and twist and scoop and block. At least that's the way the newspapers described it.

Lou decided he would be Locomotive Lou. It had a great sound. Of course, for now he'd have to be Locomotive Lou Lou, which didn't have the same ring. He often wished Maman would drop the name Lou Lou, like Papa wanted. It made him sound like a child and not a young man of twelve. It made sense for him to become Louis, not even Lou, with Georges gone. He was the number one son now. But it would have to be Lou Lou for a while longer, if he was about to become a girl. It was the only way onto this team. But could he really do it? Could he dress as a girl day and night for however long he lasted on the team and pull it off? Wouldn't he die of embarrassment if anyone he knew saw him? People admired him for being fast, but would they still admire him if they found out he was pulling a skirt over his pants? Lou knew they'd laugh and joke and tease him for the rest of his life.

I would die, he thought, as he listened to the old rooster crowing across the frozen field. *So I'll just have to make sure they never find out.*

Six

The following afternoon, Lou heard the knock at the door and the footsteps that followed. Maman would be throwing off her apron and hiding it behind a chair, sweeping back her graying hair with her fingers. Papa would be seated in his special chair under the window, but Lou could not picture his expression. Or maybe he didn't want to. Maman had spent the last half-hour talking to him in the kitchen, her voice loud enough to come through the floorboards. Lou had only been able to pick out the odd word, words like "have to" and "for your son" and "no choice." Every time Papa's voice would bounce back, his anger clear, until he'd heard Maman say the word "money." To that, Papa had had no reply. It's like the word had shut him up completely. Lou had no idea what his father made every month, but maybe it wasn't much more than the rich baker would be paying Lou.

Now he could hear Maman saying hello to Monsieur

Robichaud and leading him into the parlor to meet Papa.

Lou waited until he was sure they'd all be sitting down. So far, there had been no eruptions. That meant Papa hadn't thrown anything at the coach to make him leave. Lou had dressed carefully, in a loose-fitting sweater and the long black skirt down to his ankles. He had combed his bangs down until they hung over his face, hiding much of it. His long eyelashes were the envy of his female cousins, and Francine had told Lou she'd die for them, so that was all good.

Lou placed his feet as lightly as possible on the stairs, his heart banging against his undershirt. The smell of Maman's pea soup was heavy in the house, and it put Lou at ease. He breathed in and turned the corner into the parlor.

Monsieur Robichaud stood up as Lou entered, like he was really important.

"Ah, here is the star," he said. "I visited three towns after yours, and not one girl could skate as well as you. You are our only hope against Lapensée, my dear." From the corner of his eye, Lou saw Papa squirm when the coach said *dear*. "Your parents must be thrilled. I was just telling them about the team. We practice three times per week and have one or two games per week as well, so your skills will really improve."

"Isn't that wonderful, Papa?" said Maman.

She opened her eyes wide, as though daring Papa to disagree.

"Hmm," said Papa.

"And Lou Lou will be playing with girls from all over the province and even the country. Some of them came to Montreal to study at McGill, but they're also playing hockey with us."

Lou stiffened under his clothes. He knew what Papa thought of girls going to university, or any other kind of school. He wouldn't want Louis getting ideas in his head, even if he was a boy. Anyway, there was as little chance of a boy from his town going to university as there was for a girl. The only boys he knew who continued with school were the ones who went off to the seminary to become priests. And Lou had no intention of doing that. Priests couldn't play hockey — not for real.

"Imagine that, Alphonse," Maman said, widening her eyes at Papa again. It was like some magic spell. Every time she did it, all Papa could say was *hmm*, as though her glare had frozen his tongue. Monsieur Robichaud would think Papa was simple-minded, but Lou didn't care. As long as Papa was limited to grunting, he couldn't say the wrong thing, like Louis's name or the masculine pronoun that could give him away.

"Lou Lou will live with other girls in a respectable boarding house run by Madame Oliver, the sister of the owner of the bakery, right in the heart of the city."

Lou caught his mother making a small gesture of prayer with her hands on her lap. The word "city" had scared her. Father Béliveau was always telling people to stay away from the city. When he talked about it, Lou saw a big scary beast with sharp claws ready to rip people open or a huge mouth full of pointy teeth waiting to bite people in half, like a starved coyote. "Stay here, in the parish, where life is good and where God is watching over you," Father Béliveau said almost every Sunday. "If you are in the city, God won't be able to find you. There are too many people and too many sinners to distract Him. Here, in Saint-Christophe, He can see you clearly, like a black bear in the snow."

"You'll have some soup?" asked Maman finally.

"Madame, it smells wonderful, just like my grand-mère used to make, but I cannot. I have to get back to Montreal. There is much to do running a hockey team, even a girls' one."

"Oh yes, I am sure. We understand, don't we, Papa?"

"Hmmm."

"We'll see you on Wednesday, Lou Lou. Madame Oliver will meet you at Windsor Station. We'll have skates and a uniform all ready for you. Your maman was kind enough to tell me your sizes. Big feet for a girl, but that's okay. Big feet, big skate, right?"

Papa squirmed again, until Monsieur Robichaud reached down and shook his hand. Papa stayed glued to his seat as Maman saw their guest to the door. When they had left the room, Papa turned to Lou and said, in his gruffest voice, "Now, son, for the love of God, get out of that skirt before I kill you."

Seven

On Wednesday, Lou had to say goodbye to Papa early, before his shift at the sawmill began at seven. Lou walked his father down the hill to the end of the road, hoping he would think of something nice to say to him, but nothing came. And Papa didn't speak either. It would make leaving so much easier if Papa would say just one kind thing. Lou knew that. But, thinking back to the day Georges had left, he realized it just wasn't Papa's way. While Maman's fingers had had to be pried off Georges's shoulders, with the train wheels already starting to turn, Papa had merely shaken his hand, barely able to squeak out a sound. Maman's crying had mingled with the other mothers' sobs, filling the air like a flock of geese. Papa had spent the rest of that day out in the shed, chopping wood. It was only later, at supper, that Lou had noticed his father's eyes were ringed with red.

"Well, Papa," said Lou. "I guess I should say *salut*. You

know, I always wanted to ride the train."

"Yes, Louis, I know. Me too." Lou thought back. He had never known either of his parents to ride the train. "But I only did it one time, all the way into Montreal." This was news to Lou. He didn't know his father had been to the city.

"When, Papa?"

"When I was just about your age, Louis. With my uncle Réjean, to see Montreal beat Ottawa to win the Stanley Cup in 1894."

Lou didn't know what to say. Why had Papa never told him this before? It was incredible to think that his father had been at the first Stanley Cup game ever played.

"Wow, Papa. That must have been so exciting."

"Oh yes, it was, Louis. Especially since my parents didn't want Uncle Réjean to take me. I begged and begged, but still they said no. But my uncle was crafty. He snuck me out with him and took me anyway."

Now Lou really didn't know what to say. Papa had disobeyed his parents. And he was willing to confess this to Lou? This seemed impossible. It was almost like Papa was trying to tell him something about today, about Lou leaving. But he couldn't figure out what.

"The city is not like here, *mon fils*. You be careful." He stared at Lou for a few seconds, looking deep into his eyes, in a way he never had before. "And for a girl, it's even worse," he added. Then he held out his hand, which was still full of cuts, and Lou took it. They stood for a few seconds, until Papa released his hold. The stream let out a loud swoosh as the large wheels of the mill starting churning. It matched Papa's sigh as he turned and walked down the snow-covered hill.

Eight

Lou and Maman stood at the station, waiting for the eight o'clock train. Monsieur Geoffrion, the station master, came out of his cubbyhole when he saw them.

"Ah, *bonjour*," he said. "Alphonse told me you were off to the city today, Louis. Off to see about an apprenticeship at a bakery in Montreal, is that right?"

Lou looked at Maman to see if she knew anything about this. She nodded slightly.

"That's right, Monsieur Geoffrion," said Lou. He scanned the wall. The poster was gone. Monsieur Robichaud must have taken it down when he left town after the tryouts. Obviously Monsieur Geoffrion had not read it too closely. Luckily it had been sandwiched in between a bunch of war recruitment posters.

"Well, *bonne chance* to you. It's good to see a young man with initiative these days. And it's also good to see a young man off to something other than war, right, Angélique?" Maman nodded, and Lou was afraid she would start to cry. "Don't worry about him. The transfer in Ottawa couldn't be easier. He just has to cross the platform to the other side and wait ten minutes. He'll be fine." Monsieur Geoffrion laid his hand gently on Maman's shoulder before walking away.

Lou looked down the track. He could see the light growing brighter. A cloud of steam rose into the air along with the piercing cry of the whistle. Lou felt his mother's arms close around him.

"Now, remember what I said, *mon cher*. Be careful to get on the right train, no matter what Monsieur Geoffrion has to say. You don't want to end up in Toronto. Pop into the washroom the minute you get to the station in Montreal. Madame Oliver doesn't know what you look like, and it won't take a minute to pull the skirt over your pants and shake out your hair." Maman had made him two skirts, both with elastic at the waist, one black and one blue. She had stayed up all night knitting him a blue sweater and taking in two of her blouses. She had also sewed up a flannel nightgown.

"I'll write to you, Maman."

"No, don't. We'd have to ask Monsieur Geoffrion to read your letters to us, and we can't do that, can we?"

"Ask Francine. She knows, Maman." Lou had called on her last night to say goodbye.

"You made some of the girls look bad and you took away their chances. Just like a boy," she'd said.

"I didn't mean to, Francine. I mean, that's not why I

did it. Besides, you're the one who dared me. And you could have come. I didn't ruin it for you."

"But you still get to go and I don't, just because you're a boy. And if he hadn't chosen you, he might have asked one of the other girls who could go, like Paulette. I will never speak to you again, Lou."

They had been out on the ice, doing laps.

"Never?" asked Lou.

"Never," said Francine. But then she took his hand, and they spent the next hour skating round and round just like they had done many times before. It had proved what Lou had always known: out on the ice, everything was forgiven.

The train let out a blast of hot steam at their feet. Lou grabbed his bag and threw it over his shoulder. Maman grabbed his face. If she kissed him on the mouth he would die of embarrassment. He could see strangers in the train windows, watching them on the platform.

"Take care, Lou Lou," said Maman, kissing his cheeks.

"I will, Maman," said Lou, pulling back. Now that the train was here, he couldn't wait to get away from his small town and ride into the big, dangerous city.

Nine

⬤

M any hours later, when Lou was on the second, bigger train, they crossed a heavy iron bridge over the river and onto the island of Montreal. Lou had learned that Montreal was an island at school, from Brother Simon, his teacher for the last seven years. Out the window to his left, Lou watched the Lake of Two Mountains open up, its choppy waters swirling under the tracks. Everything about the ride was exciting. Suddenly, away from home, even what he was about to try to do became exciting and not just scary. Still, the whole trip his mind was doing somersaults. When he thought about living as a girl day after day he could feel cold sweat breaking out around his underarms and down his back. He was pretty sure girls didn't sweat that way. Then he would think about playing hockey on a real team in a real arena, and playing against some of the best players — even if they were girls — and the excitement would come back.

He tried not to think about the fact that what he was going to do was dishonest. He knew what Father Béliveau would have to say about fooling people and cheating them through lying. Yet somehow, on the grand scale of lying and cheating, putting on a skirt in order to play hockey didn't seem that bad. The only person Lou could hurt doing this was himself. But he could hurt himself very badly.

Lou looked at the man across the aisle and suddenly had the crazy idea of asking him what he thought of Lou's plan, but the man had been reading the *Montreal Star*, an English newspaper, the whole ride down and probably wouldn't understand him. Besides, did the English have the same ideas about these things? He really didn't know.

Lou took a deep breath and watched the bare trees flow by the window. It seemed like the train was standing still and the land was moving. Lou went backwards in his mind to the day before Georges had left for the war. They had been skating on the lake, doing laps, gaining speed each time around. The bare trees whipped past in the corner of their vision. They didn't talk, but Lou knew they were both thinking the same thing: how one day they would be skating like that on a big team. It was their dream. Lou knew Georges had taken that dream with him to Europe. Now he thought of Georges and the other soldiers and what they might be doing in Belgium. Or what someone else might be doing to them. But the thought of anything bad happening to Georges was too much, especially today, when he had so much else to worry about.

Minutes later the train slipped into a dark tunnel, its pace slowing down. They must be coming to the station. All around him people were pulling down their luggage and gathering their things, so Lou did the same. His plan was to walk as close as possible behind a tall person, then dash to the washroom.

The English man was very tall. Papa said English people were taller because they liked looking down at French Canadians, but this man barely noticed Lou, which was perfect. Lou stood a step behind him and walked with his head down, off the train, onto the platform and up the stairs into the station. He didn't look right or left. He followed the English man like he was his servant or his tiny shadow. What luck! The man was heading straight for the washroom that had a large round light with a picture of a man on it.

The right wall was lined with urinals. Lou had never peed in front of other men before, at least not in a wash-room, only out in the woods amongst friends. Thank God there were a few stalls. Lou ran into one, locked the door, and quickly pulled on the skirt and kicked off his pants. He then fluffed up his hair and pinched his cheeks like his maman had shown him, to make them pink. For some reason, girls always had pink cheeks. He threw his hat on his head to push down his bangs.

Ready or not, he had to go. What would Madame Oliver be thinking? Maybe she'd leave and then what would he do? He didn't have her address or phone number, if she even had a telephone. The only one Lou had ever seen was in the small train station at home.

But when Lou stepped out of the stall, three men were standing at the urinals, doing their business. All heads turned toward him as he ran past.

"Hey, young lady," one called out. "What are you trying to do, give us all a heart attack? This is the men's."

He could hear them laughing and calling as he ran out the door, and he felt his cheeks burning. What had he done? He wasn't thinking. For the first time, it struck Lou that he was actually going out in public dressed as a girl. Maybe it wasn't going to be as easy as he'd thought. Not only that, but he'd have to be way more careful. He'd have to think about every move he made.

He hadn't been in Montreal ten minutes and he'd almost blown it.

Ten

ou emerged from the washroom and took a minute
to look around. This place was magnificent, with
high stone walls, marble floors, and gold fixtures. He
felt like he was in a palace. A tall, elegantly dressed
woman was standing near the stairs he had come up a
few minutes earlier, looking left and right, like she was
expecting someone. Could this be his chaperone? He
pulled back his shoulders and slowed his pace, taking
smaller steps. Francine had told him girls didn't take
such huge strides, once she had started talking to him
again. He'd have to remember that, and all the other
advice she'd given him out on the ice before he left.

"Madame Oliver?" he said.

"Lou Lou? Oh my, where did you come from? I was
starting to worry. Monsieur Robichaud said you were
a quiet one. I didn't even see you coming."

"I'm sorry. I had to go to the washroom." Well, it
wasn't a lie.

"Okay, let's go. I have a car waiting."

A car! This would be Lou's first real car ride. He and Francine had sat in one once, at the train station, when no one was looking. It must have belonged to someone who had come to do business at the sawmill. But he had never ridden in one.

Out on the street, Lou's mouth fell open. All around him were tall buildings. Cars, horses and buggies, and people all moved together between them. It seemed like everyone was in a rush. He had worried that people would notice him and point and whisper, but no one even looked his way. He was like a tiny ant in this crowd. He had an impulse to grab Madame Oliver's hand so he wouldn't get lost. But what would she think? Monsieur Robichaud had said Lou would be the youngest on the team. Normally he didn't take anyone under fourteen, but Lou had such talent. Maybe Madame Oliver would just think he was a baby.

She sat beside him on the high-backed seat. The driver nodded, then moved to the front of the car and turned the crank. The engine sputtered and began to chug. The driver jumped in and steered the car smoothly away from the curb. *If only I could write to Georges*, Lou thought. *He'd be so amazed to hear about this.*

The car twisted and turned through busy streets until they were in a quieter neighborhood. Trees hung over the roads like an archway, touching in the middle. Out the window to his right Lou saw a mountain.

"That is Mount Royal," Madame Oliver said. "Pretty, isn't it? You'll see the cross at nighttime." Now Lou remembered Brother Simon talking about the famous cross on Mount Royal. Somewhere near it was a big church called Saint Joseph's Oratory.

"You'll see it all in time, Lou Lou, with the other girls." This time, when she spoke, Lou noticed a trace of an English accent. Maybe Papa was wrong. Maybe some English people could speak French. He didn't want to ask her. He was trying not to say much. He had decided it was best to establish himself as someone who spoke little. Monsieur Robichaud had already started that rumor. If he continued it, it would be easier not to say something wrong. Besides, he felt a bit silly every time he talked in that low whisper, like it wasn't his own voice.

Finally the car stopped beside a tall stone house with a wooden door at the top of a wide staircase.

"We're here, Lou Lou," said Madame Oliver.

Lou took a deep breath. Behind the upstairs windows, three girls looked down on him. His stomach roiled. Three girls! Would they really accept him as number four?

And would he really be able to accept himself?

Eleven

"Everyone, come meet Lou Lou," called Madame Oliver, removing her feathered hat and laying it over a hook on a carved wooden stand in the hallway. "You can leave your coat here, on this hook."

The sound of three girls running down the stairs shook the chandelier over Lou's head. It was an electric one, not gas or candle. Lou had never flicked a light switch before. He wondered if he'd be allowed to flick this one, in time.

"Girls, girls," said Madame Oliver. "You're not at the rink now. Remember what we talked about? Boys on the rink, girls at home. I expect perfect ladylike behavior at all times. You know what most people think about girls playing hockey. We have to prove them wrong. You'll have no trouble with that, Lou Lou, I can tell." She smiled at him, showing the most perfect white teeth he had ever seen. He cringed inside. Was he really ladylike? What would Papa say if he heard that?

Suddenly the girls were all around him, like they wanted to pick him apart, the way the chickens at home circled around the crust ends of Maman's molasses bread. They said their names all at once, so that all he heard was a blur of syllables.

Madame Oliver clapped. "Against the wall, everyone. Not you, Lou Lou. You come stand by me."

The girls did as they were told, standing with their hands behind their backs, trying not to giggle.

"Lou Lou, I present to you Claire, Bernadette, and Danielle. Everyone, this is Lou Lou." One by one the girls curtsied or waved. They wore their hair loose, floating over their shoulders. They had sparkling eyes of various colors, and they smiled at him as if he were a treasure.

Lou was sure they would see the sweat breaking out on his forehead and palms.

"We've heard so much about you from Monsieur Robichaud," said Claire, who was the prettiest of the girls. She had clear blue-green eyes, the color of the lake at home in summer.

"Coach says you're the best skater he's ever seen," said Bernadette.

"He says you'll save us," said Danielle. "Well, you and Claire." She looked at Claire and smiled. Lou thought he detected some annoyance in Claire's expression.

"I play right wing," Claire said. "But how can I be a strong winger without a strong center? I'll be very happy if you turn out to be that perfect center."

All Lou could do was nod. He was afraid he'd stammer if he tried to speak. He had never been paid so much attention by three pretty girls all at once. For the second time since getting off the train at Windsor Station, Lou worried about pulling this off. He hadn't given a moment's thought to how hard it would be to be surrounded by girls, how it would make his heart race and his knees quiver.

"Show her the room. Help her get settled," ordered Madame Oliver. "Lunch in ten minutes."

Claire pulled Lou up the stairs by the hand, the other two pushing from behind. It was like they couldn't stop touching him. Francine was right. Girls were different! A group of boys would never swarm him like this or actually touch him. How could he tell them not to?

"We have these two rooms," said Claire. "I've been alone for weeks, while Danielle and Bernadette share that one. Some nights they let me in, other nights they don't. But now I won't need them because I'll have you." She linked her arm around Lou's and pulled him into the room they would share. He sighed with relief when he saw two small beds, one against each wall, with a small table between them.

"We pushed *our* beds together," said Bernadette. "Danielle and I. We like them like that. It makes it easier to talk after lights out. Madame Oliver is very fussy about lights out. Nine o'clock on weeknights, can you imagine?"

Claire was looking at him intently, as if waiting to see if he wanted to do that too.

"I think I prefer to sleep like this," he said, hoping she wouldn't take offense. "For now, at least."

"We heard you were shy. Don't worry. We'll soon be like sisters. Let me help you unpack," said Claire. Lou couldn't remember what was in his suitcase. Was there something there that could give him away? Yes, there was. There definitely was. It was the thing that would save him on the ice. He couldn't let Claire find it.

"It's okay. I'll do it after lunch. I'm starving," said Lou, shoving the suitcase under the bed. "Where is the washroom, please?"

"Down there," pointed Danielle. "And we all four have to share it, so the rule is no locking unless you absolutely have to."

Lou felt himself sinking faster and faster. Perhaps he should just confess now and take the evening train back home. But then Madame Oliver called and everyone ran back downstairs while Lou popped into the wash-room. It was huge, with white tiles everywhere, even on the walls. The bath was so deep he might be able to swim in it. A bottle of bubble bath stood on the rim, in a silver tray, and although he had never used bubble bath in his life, he knew that might come in handy for hiding.

He splashed water on his face and fluffed up his hair. Then he used the toilet, which had a pull chain above it for flushing. What would Madame Oliver think if she saw their outhouse back home, with its deep, dark hole?

He washed his hands, using soap shaped like a rose. He turned at the door before leaving and gasped. He had left the seat up. He was pretty sure a girl wouldn't lift the seat to pee.

He ran back and flicked it down just as Claire appeared. He'd have to remember to do these small things. Maybe he'd have to learn to pee sitting down, to be safe.

"There you are, Lou Lou. We thought you'd gotten lost. Come on." She took his hand, squeezed it, and didn't let go. He had to work hard at not pulling his hand back or showing his embarrassment. The whole situation was becoming much more difficult than he had imagined. And he'd only just arrived in Montreal.

Francine's face came to him, the night before he left. She had kissed him, out on the ice. Georges had told him you could tell if a kiss was real by whether the girl's eyes were open or closed. Francine's had been shut tight. That meant it was real. And Lou had liked it.

She would not like to see him with Claire right now.

Twelve

After Lou had unpacked, the three girls begged Madame Oliver to be allowed to take him on a walk around the neighborhood.

"*Très bien*," she replied. "But be back by three. Monsieur Robichaud is coming, and then we're off to the rink." Lou's ears pricked up at the word "rink." That was why he was here, after all.

The walk was a kind of torture, as the girls pointed out curtains and dresses, assessing their styles and colors. "Oh, look at them," Claire said. She stopped and pointed at two women with dead foxes wrapped around their necks.

"They must be very rich," Bernadette said.

"Richer than Madame Oliver," Danielle added. Lou, Papa, and Georges had all shot foxes before. How funny it would be to watch Maman wrap the pelt around her neck instead of using it to make winter hats. Some of the fashionable women they passed were no older than

Francine. He thought of Francine and all the work she had to do at home, washing clothes and floors, cooking, and scrubbing pots. How she would love to be here with them, taking a leisurely stroll in a fancy coat, her hands tucked inside a furry roll.

Lou decided to steer the conversation to hockey.

"What positions do the rest of you play?" he asked as they entered a park where people were walking dogs.

"Monsieur Robichaud makes us do everything," Danielle said. "But I am best at defense." She ran ahead on the path and puffed herself out so that she was suddenly bigger, the way Lou had seen birds do. "Come on, just try to get past." Lou didn't know how much strength he should show. There were snowbanks on either side, so he'd have to ram through her, but she was quick. He tried darting left to right, and she matched him move for move. He put his head down and pushed, but she held him back with strong arms. Maybe he could push harder, but he decided not to. Not today at least.

"See? She *is* the best," said Bernadette, and then she and Danielle clasped hands and spun round and round on the path, releasing and flying into opposite snowbanks. Their high-pitched laughter soared into the sky. Lou supposed this was just the type of scene Madame Oliver would not want to see in public. And neither would Father Béliveau, who had once called on Francine's parents to talk about how much time she spent on the lake skating with Lou in winter. It wasn't so much that she was skating — it was the way she skated. To try to beat Lou, she had to hike her skirt up as high as she could, bunched in her fists. Most of the time, they'd both end up in a snowbank on the other side.

On the way back, each girl told him where she was from. All small towns, expect for Claire, who had grown up in an orphanage in Quebec City. "I never knew my parents. I grew up with the nuns. The only fun thing they ever let us do was skate. Some of the brothers from the abbé would make us a rink in the backyard every winter. They'd come over and play hockey a few times a week, and they let me play with them, even though the sisters didn't approve. Even without the brothers I would skate for hours, until the sun went down and my toes were frozen. Sister Clothilde, my favorite, even prayed for me. She said I skated like someone possessed. She talked about bringing me to St. Joseph's in Montreal to be cured by Brother André, like I was sick or something."

"And now here you are with us," said Danielle. "Our best skater. No offense, Lou Lou."

"Imagine," said Bernadette. "We are all here, alone, in Montreal. Some girls my age are already getting married back home. They'll have kids soon. We're so lucky."

The word "lucky" was like a signal to huddle, arms around each other's shoulders, and bounce. Lou had to join in, even though he felt ridiculous springing up and down on his toes in his worn lace-up boots, hand-me-downs from Georges. The funny thing was, he could relate to the idea of luck. Not that he'd be getting married or having kids any time soon — Georges would do that first — but he did feel that he had escaped something too. He'd been given a chance to do something different and incredible. He didn't mind holding Claire's hand as they ran back to the rooming house, slowing only when they were at the corner, in case Madame Oliver was watching.

I am not the only one with things to hide, thought Lou.

Thirteen

Monsieur Robichaud had a car too, so the girls split up, two by two, and met down at Victoria Rink. There the rest of the girls were waiting, already lacing up their skates. Lou walked behind Madame Oliver, too awed by the sight of the rink to hurry. He knew that this was the rink where the first indoor hockey game had been played. The huge ice surface was surrounded by a wide wooden platform where people strolled around, watching the skaters. The ceiling was formed of arched wooden beams that met in the middle like the roofs of the churches Brother Simon had shown them pictures of in class. He looked up, expecting to see Jesus hanging there on the cross, blessing all the skaters.

"Everyone, this is Lou Lou," Monsieur Robichaud announced to the two groups of girls who were standing around on the ice, leaning on their sticks. "She is a great skater, one of the best I've seen, and I expect she's going to add a lot to the team." The girls all nodded in Lou's direction, and when they started to talk he noticed that one group spoke English and the other French. The English girls must have been the McGill girls Coach had talked about back home.

"Laps everyone, laps. Without delay. As many as you can." The girls took off. Lou was about to throw on his old skates, which were so worn he could see through to his socks, when Monsieur Robichaud handed him a brand new pair made of shiny black leather. "We can't have you skating in those," he said.

They fit perfectly and were so much better than his old ones, which were hand-me-downs from Georges. They held his ankles upright, and the blades shone like silver.

On the ice, Lou raced to catch up with the other girls. He looked for Claire, who was way ahead. She really was a good skater. It was only the second time he had skated in a skirt, and he had forgotten how annoying it was to have that large swath of material constantly restraining his legs. Then he noticed that some of the other girls weren't in long skirts. Their skirts were short, blooming out around their thighs then gathering at the knee. They looked so much more comfortable. If only he'd known to ask Maman to make him a skirt like that.

The Montreal Bakers were not alone on the ice. The rink was full of people, old and young, some skating slowly, others spinning around. That meant Lou had to zigzag around other skaters, careful not to knock anyone down. But that was what a real game was like, wasn't it?

Coach blew his whistle, and all the Bakers skated back to their corner of the rink.

"Ladies, our next game Saturday night is against the best. I know I don't have to tell you all who that is."

"The Cornwall Vics," shouted Bernadette.

"That's right. And do I have to remind you who is on that team?"

"Albertine Lapensée," shouted several girls at once. Then they all sucked in their breath and let out a long boo.

"Each and every one of you is going to have to play your very best to help us win that game."

Coach Robichaud stopped and looked each girl square in the face. They met his stare without flinching, not like the girls at home, who looked down a lot. "Now, we're going to do drills around the rink today. I want you to skate your fastest and not lose the puck, not even for a second. I'm going to time you. The fastest forwards will start the game. Lou Lou, as our newest player, you go first, with Claire and Alice."

Coach repeated his instructions in English for Alice, then pulled out a puck and a stopwatch, the same one he'd had on the rink back home. Lou lined up between the other two girls. They didn't look at each other once, and Lou could feel the tension between them, like they were on different teams. "Ready? Go."

Lou took off. He tried his best to ignore the skirt and pretend he was back in his knee-length pants. The puck danced on the end of his stick, as though it were held there by magic. Flick flick, back and forth, left and right. At one point he even slipped it between a couple who were holding hands, dipped around them, and picked it up. He was about to turn back and stick his tongue out at them until he remembered it wasn't the sort of thing a girl would do. Claire and Alice were keeping up with him, but they hadn't passed him. He could see them from the corners of his eyes, approaching the turn. Lou wasn't used to playing hockey on a rink with boards. All of his hockey playing had been on the lake, where piled snow served as the borders. He didn't even think of doing what Claire had just done. She had hit the puck into the corner and was skating around to meet it. Alice was doing the same to his left. He'd have to practice that move. Finally he let up a fine spray of ice as he ground to a halt beside the Bakers, seconds after Claire, but before Alice.

"Fifty-five seconds," said Coach. "Impressive, Claire. Not bad Lou Lou, at fifty-seven. Sixty for you, Alice." The girls around them clapped, and a few slapped Claire on the back. The McGill girls glared at Lou like they weren't impressed at all. "Okay, everyone now. Do the same, only three times around."

They continued practicing for an hour, ending with a drill where they passed the puck between pairs as best they could with so many other skaters on the ice. Lou hooked up with Claire. They passed the puck back and forth effortlessly. She matched him pass for pass, like they were one another's shadows. He followed her lead in the corners and learned how to shoot the puck ahead against the boards. Claire had it worked out to a science. She could hit any target on the board and make the puck bounce back to exactly where she wanted. The rink the brothers had put in behind her orphanage must have had similar boards.

"Good work out there, Lou Lou," she said to him later. He didn't know why, but he felt a great sense of relief.

"You too, Claire." Lou couldn't help thinking that if Lapensée was actually better than Claire, she must be very good. Working with Claire hadn't been easy.

At the end of the practise, Coach pulled out a dollar and told them all to skate over to the canteen for an ice cream cone.

In his head, Lou added it to the list of things to tell Maman.

Fourteen

That night and the next morning, Lou insisted on changing in the washroom. And he made sure to lock the door, loudly. It was what he had decided he needed to do. He didn't care if it made him seem strange, or even standoffish. Now that the coach had presented him as a great skater and someone who could help the team, he was hoping the girls at Madame Oliver's would cut him some slack. He made sure he was extra friendly with them the rest of the time. And it seemed to work.

"It's kind of cute that you're so shy," said Claire.

"Yeah, it's old-fashioned," added Bernadette.

"Maybe it's just how she was raised," he overheard Danielle tell the others out in the hallway. "We have to respect it."

"It's true. And don't forget she has no sisters, only one brother. My six sisters and I always changed together. We even bathed together. Lou Lou didn't have that," Bernadette replied.

"Where I grew up, there was no such thing as privacy. We were fifty girls in one big dorm. We knew everything about everyone. There was nowhere to hide a thing." Lou sensed that Claire was staring past the locked bathroom door to where he stood, half naked, and it made him shiver.

The first time Claire sat on his bed and told him to move over he said no. "But Madame Oliver will hear us talking if we have to shout across the room," Claire said.

"No, she won't. And I don't like anyone in bed with me," Lou said. "I'm just not used to it. Remember? I'm the only girl at home." He remembered her words from earlier. "Sorry."

"Oh, yeah. Poor Lou Lou." Then she leaned over him and kissed him on the cheek and ran her hand through his hair. His entire body flushed, like a log suddenly picking up the flames from kindling. He turned away, toward the wall, so that Claire wouldn't notice, and held his body still so that she wouldn't hear how fast his heart was racing.

"Good night, Lou Lou," called Claire. Then he listened to her kneel on the floor beside her bed and say her prayers, blessing all the kids back in the orphanage and many of the sisters. Sister Clothilde got the most attention; Claire asked God to especially watch out for her. The whole process took her a good ten minutes. Lou supposed she had learned to do this in the orphanage. The sisters would have expected it. Maman prayed every night, but she had given up expecting Lou and Georges to do it too.

The Bakers actually got the ice to themselves early Saturday morning, so they could set up a net and put in their goalie, Magdalène, a large-framed girl from Chicoutimi who claimed she was related to Georges Vézina. She was good. Lou could only score on her six out of twelve times that he carried the puck down from center ice.

An hour before the game against the Vics was set to start, Madame Oliver came in carrying a large stack of clothing. "New uniforms," she announced. "New player, new start, new uniforms." She held up a bright red sweater with a large silver "B" sewn onto the chest. Then she held up one of those short skirts some of the girls already wore, black with a red band around the bottom. But wait! Now that she swooshed it around, Lou could see that it was not a skirt. It was sewn in half in the middle, like a weird pair of balloon shorts. He'd be able to move even better now that it was closer to what he should be wearing. The last pieces of the uniform were bright red leggings and a bright red tuque with a pompom on top.

"Everyone, come get one of each," Madame Oliver said. "We have small, medium, and large." The girls all ran to the heap and started pulling out pieces. Then they hopped onto the benches that sat around them in the small changing room and started pulling off their old clothes to change.

Lou froze. What was he going to do? Would he blow it before playing his first real game? From the waist up he could possibly pass for a girl, one slow to develop, but not below that, not even with the loose underwear he wore over his jockstrap.

He pulled out a size small of everything and braced the bundle under his arm. He swallowed hard, then said to Madame Oliver, "Is there a washroom near here, please?"

"Oh, Lou Lou," she said, putting her hand on his shoulder like she pitied him. "I forgot how shy you are. Come with me." She took his hand and led him around the corner.

In the stall, Lou stepped out of his old leggings. He stared down at his underwear and gulped hard. None of this was going to be easy.

Fifteen

"Lou Lou," said Coach. "You, Claire, and Bernadette are the opening line. You skated fastest.
Don't let us down."

This is what Lou had come for, but his knees shook
as he skated to center ice. He tried to focus downward,
but the large crowd that filled every square inch of the
boardwalk was so noisy and restless, he just couldn't
forget they were there. Hundreds of people, all there
to watch girls play hockey. If Papa and Father Béliveau
were here, they'd be so surprised. Or maybe the priest
was right. People were here because they were curious,
not because they expected good hockey.

As Lou waited for the Vics to set up, he thought about
Georges, hiding in his trench so far away. If only he
hadn't volunteered to go off to war. He could be here
watching too. But wait a minute! If Georges and all
the other boys hadn't left for war in Europe, they'd be
the ones playing. There's no way so many girls' teams

would have popped up if the boys had been home. And Lou would be back in Saint-Christophe, using frozen cow turds as pucks, dreaming of Montreal.

The referee, wearing a black-and-white striped jersey, skated over. Lou didn't dare look into his eyes. What if there was a male gaze that all men could spot, something that would give him away? He kept his eyes glued to the circle at his feet.

Where was Lapensée? He couldn't wait to face her. He couldn't wait to show her what a real hockey player could do. What a boy could do, even though only he would know that a boy had beaten her. He reminded himself that this was why he had come: to beat Lapensée. After he'd done that, he could leave. But the thought of leaving this magnificent rink tore at him. He'd have to think about everything later, after the game.

No sooner had he thought that than a girl skated to center ice, fast. She skidded to a sideways halt, spraying Lou from head to toe. He could taste the ice in his mouth and feel it dripping from his lashes. And he could hear the crowd laughing. Even the referee chuckled as he said, "Okay, Albertine. A little sportsmanship, all right?"

Lapensée slapped her stick on the ice and leaned into it. She was big, way bigger than Lou was expecting. Her eyes and hair were dark, her shoulders broad. For a horrible second, Lou wondered if her real name was Albert and she too was pretending, just like him. She

looked way more masculine than Lou. Even her eyebrows stretched across her forehead and met in the
middle, thick as a moustache.

The referee blew the whistle, and the crowd let out a
roar. Lapensée didn't even try to win the puck. Instead
she rammed right through Lou, knocking him to the
ice. "Take that, you little runt," she hollered as she
zoomed past him with the puck. Lou watched Bernadette, who was playing left wing, rush in to try to stop
her. Up ahead, Danielle was ready for Lapensée, skating
backwards in front of her and throwing her shoulder
into the star.

So this was women's hockey? Lou had pictured
dainty passes floating slowly across the ice and players
who glided around, pushing the puck forward without
leaning over. He had pictured himself sticking out, the
only one on the ice who could speed around and control
the puck. Had he ever been wrong.

All around him girls were grunting and flying, pushing each other out of the way to get the puck. And when
they had it, they carried it long distances, weaving and
passing. By the time he'd gotten over the shock, Lapensée
was ripping the puck into the net. Magdalène, the goalie
from Chicoutimi, didn't even see it coming.

"Go, Lou Lou, go!" Lou heard from the team bench.
It was Coach, urging him on. Three minutes into the first
period and he had barely moved his legs. It was already
1–0 Cornwall. Monsieur Robichaud would be putting

him on the train tomorrow anyway if he didn't come to life.

As Lou sat on the bench watching the McGill line play against the Vics, he remembered that poster at the train station, how it had boasted that Albertine Lapensée was a hockey sensation, better than any other female player and just as good as many men. He remembered how he had laughed and prickled inside, how badly he had wanted to prove that poster wrong, no matter what.

When Coach tapped his shoulder to send him back out, his legs jumped into action and he took off toward Lapensée, who had the puck and was heading down for another shot. Danielle stood in her way, ready to stop her. But before Lapensée reached the defense, Lou zoomed in front of her and scooped the puck away. He was halfway back up the ice now, his eyes glued to the Cornwall net. Every second another foul word, the kind that would have Maman reaching for the soap, hit his ears. He used them to push himself forward. He heard Claire to his right, urging him to pass her the puck. Should he trust her? The Vics' defense were closing in on him, so he did. Claire kept up with him, and just when a defenseman was about to hit her, she passed the puck back to Lou. It wasn't the most precise pass, sailing a foot past his stick, but he lunged forward and picked it up. Within seconds two girls bumped him, one on either side, sandwiching him between them. But they couldn't stop him. He sent the puck ahead and jumped over them to retrieve it. He could feel Lapensée behind him, breathing dragon fire down his neck. He wound up and smashed the puck with all his force.

The crowd cheered as the puck sailed high into the right corner.

It was the type of cheer Lou had heard in his dreams.

But he gloated for too long. The referee had dropped the puck and Lapensée was already across center ice, on her way to her second goal. By the time Lou was close enough to steal the puck away, she was winding up. But Magdalène was ready this time. Lou could see that. Her arms were out to either side, her legs wide. Danielle was ready too. Lou laughed as she shot her right hip into Lapensée's side, sending her off balance. The crowd cheered, but Lapensée was unstoppable. She recovered her balance and regained the puck. This time, she skated close to the net. She deked right, then left, and simply slid the puck between the goalie's legs.

It was 3–1 Cornwall after twenty minutes.

Lou sat with his teammates on the bench, stunned. Coach was pacing above them.

"You need to get the puck, girls. Don't let Lapensée have all the fun. Don't be scared to challenge her. Bernadette, good try. Lou Lou, it's your first game, but don't give up. Keep doing what you did to score. Alice and Violet, work as a team. You can't give this team ten seconds down time. You saw what they'll do with it. They'll kill you. Now get back out there and make the bakery proud."

What Lou couldn't confess was that he was sore from head to toe, and so tired he just wanted to curl up on the bench and sleep. This was the hardest hockey he had ever played in his life. The last two periods were just as tough. Lou tried and tried, taking and giving perfect passes to both Claire and Bernadette, but they could only put the puck in the net once, off Claire's stick. The McGill girls tried their best too. Coach alternated between two French lines and one English line, three minutes each, but Lapensée hardly took a break. She was like a machine. Lou thought she must have a coal hatch somewhere on her back and when she sat on the bench the coach shoveled more lumps in.

The final score sat thick and heavy in Lou's stomach all night long, 5–2 for Cornwall. Lapensée had scored all of her team's goals.

It wasn't the start Lou had been hoping for.

Sixteen

"Sundays are days of rest," declared Madame Oliver at breakfast the next morning. The girls were all eating quietly, and no one had mentioned last night's game yet. "No girl living under my roof will go near a rink on Sundays. Today, girls, is the day for two things: church and culture. Go put on your best."

As they climbed the stairs, Danielle tried to cheer everyone up by reminding them that they were still getting used to each other. "Claire and Bernadette have played together, but not with you, Lou Lou. It takes time to adjust."

"Let's hope," said Claire. "Now, Lou Lou, what nice things did you bring to wear?"

So far, Lou had been lucky. When not at the rink he simply wore one of the long skirts Maman had made him and an old hockey sweater. But today he knew he'd have to do better. Maman had given him one of her older blouses, with a lace collar high around the neck. She had taken it in on the sides, keeping it a little loose around the chest to hide his flatness.

"Not much," he said. He carried Maman's clothes into the bathroom and locked the door. A few minutes later, he looked at himself in the long mirror on the back of the bathroom door. The sight of himself dressed up fancy, like a real girl, made him want to roar. He longed to rip everything off and pull on his trousers and run out of the house, taking the stairs two at a time. How fun it would be to spend the day as a boy.

That's when he thought of it. He took a washcloth and ran it under the hot water tap, another luxury that he wished Maman could have at home. Then he held it to his forehead and cheeks, pressing until his skin turned red.

"Madame Oliver, do you think I might stay home today? I'm suddenly not feeling very well," he said from the middle of the grand staircase. The girls were all gathered on the porch, putting on their coats. They were already used to Lou being last.

"Oh, my dear. You do look red. Is your throat sore?"

"Yes, it is." He tried to make his voice sound gravelly.

"Then you must rest. I'll have Céline bring you up some soup at lunch. Go back to bed. We'll see you around two o'clock."

"Thank you, madame. I'm really sorry I can't come. Have a fun day," Lou said. Then he turned and walked slowly up the stairs, coughing as he climbed.

As soon as the front door was shut, he tore off the girl clothes and jumped into the trousers and sweater he had worn on the trip here. He loved the way they felt, so loose and non-constricting. And they hadn't been washed since he left home, so they had a wonderful scent of sweat. Male sweat, built up by running and chopping wood.

But wait a minute, a voice in his head proclaimed. *Girls sweat too. You know because you've seen it and smelled it.* Lou had tried his best not to stare at the girls after he'd changed out of his hockey uniform yesterday. He thought he'd taken forever to get changed in the washroom, but the girls were even slower. It seemed they liked to linger, half-dressed, showing off the sweat stains on their undershirts and the bruises on their legs.

"If our mothers could see us now," Danielle had said. "Sorry, Claire," she'd added when she saw Claire's face. "Or if Sister Clothilde could see you."

Lou had been thankful for the undershirts that hid the brassieres and underpants he knew the girls were wearing. His face would have been scarlet if those had been exposed.

He waited until he was sure he heard the maid banging around in the kitchen, then he tiptoed back down the stairs. Céline was singing, the way his maman did when she cooked. He counted to three then ran, closing the front door softly behind him.

Seventeen

Lou had no idea where to go, so he just walked, following the downtown crowds, passing several streetcars as he did. How he wished he had the money for a ticket. It would be such fun to clutch a rail and pull himself on board, to squish himself in amongst all the people. He liked the thought that nobody would know him. He could do whatever he wanted, and it wouldn't get back to Papa and Maman like it would at home. He passed many enormous churches and wondered which one Madame Oliver and the girls were at. Imagine if they came out and walked right by him.

He followed the biggest groups of people and ended up at Place Jacques Cartier. It seemed like everyone in the city was there, strolling in their Sunday best along the cobblestoned streets. A few women were carrying umbrellas, even though it wasn't raining. His mother would laugh. She didn't even own an umbrella. When it rained she simply tied a kerchief over her head. These umbrellas had ruffles around the rim, and Lou decided they must be to keep off the sun. Claire had told him that city girls were awfully concerned about getting sun on their faces, even in winter. They wanted their skin to be milky white.

At the bottom of the square the river opened up, running fast and wide. Lou saw dozens of ships and wondered what it would be like to sail up the St. Lawrence River and across the Atlantic Ocean, like Georges and his mates had done. Men were passing boxes down from some of the ships to other men standing on the wharf.

"Hey, kid," a large man called over. "Wanna make a dime?" Lou looked behind him.

"No, you," the man repeated, pointing at Lou. "Come help us."

Lou wanted that dime. He was being well looked after at Madame Oliver's, but he had no money of his own. If he had his own dime he could go back to that stand where those wieners were roasting on charcoal. The smell had made his mouth water. At Madame Oliver's he was conscious of trying not to eat like he normally did at home. Papa liked to call him *petit cochon* — little pig — because of the way he didn't come up for air. But here, at the boarding house, he copied Claire and the other girls, taking daintier bites and making sure to stay straight-backed while he chewed. The food had to find his mouth, not the other way around.

"What's your name?" the man asked, heaving a box above his head.

"Lou, monsieur."

"Okay, Lou, you can call me Boss. Understand?"

Lou became part of a chain of men, somewhere in the middle between ship and shore. He was one of six, just like a hockey team. Each person had to do his part in order for the whole operation to work. Except if one of those people was Albertine Lapensée. She could do it all herself. Lou tried to stop thinking about how little he had done yesterday, apart from scoring that first goal. The whole pace of the game had surprised him so much that he couldn't get moving. It had been like he was on the boardwalk watching the action instead of out on the ice, taking part in it. Even though Coach Robichaud had not said anything to him directly after the game, Lou could tell he was disappointed. He had expected more from his new player.

"We need to move this stuff fast," Boss said. "Christmas is around the corner, men. That's where we make our money."

Lou wondered what lay inside the wooden boxes his hands were now grabbing, their weight adding to the soreness of his muscles. Could it be ornaments, like the ones he'd seen on some of the houses and shops? At home they strung dried berries and made garlands of pine branches. There was an endless supply of those. But imagine being able to buy Maman a silver globe with a picture of baby Jesus in the manger painted on it. He'd even seen ones that were carved out, so that you could place a candle inside and make the image glow. Maman's face would light up, too, if she had one.

The boxes were soon unloaded.

"Thank you, son," said Boss, handing him a shiny dime. "Good work. You're stronger than you look. Hey, Jacques, check this kid out." Before he knew it, the man was lifting Lou over his shoulders and tossing him up in the air to the next man on the chain. On and on he was tossed, his large Sunday breakfast rolling around in his stomach. When he came to the foot of the ship, the man who was holding him passed him up to the man on board.

He couldn't believe it. There he was, standing on the deck of a tall ship. He looked up to the top of the masts and imagined climbing them to fix the sails or to look out for land. His number-one wish was to play hockey, but right now, standing there with the cold breeze coming in off the water, he knew that sailing around the world would be exciting too.

The sailor smiled and tossed Lou another dime. "Thanks, kid," he said. "Now get going." He kicked Lou in the bum and laughed as Lou was forced to jump down. Oh God! If he twisted an ankle, what would he tell Madame Oliver? How could you twist an ankle lying in bed?

But he didn't. He landed on a pile of soft snow.

Clutching the dimes, he ran all the way back up Beaver Hall Hill and along rue Sainte-Catherine to Mackay, then up to Simpson, his new street. By the time he undressed and changed into his flannel nightgown, he was hot and sweaty. Perfect. Céline brought the soup up to him a few minutes later.

"You are sick, *ma chérie*," she said. "You're burning up. My famous chicken soup will save you. All of Saint-Hyacinthe was once rescued by my soup. Believe me." Céline sounded just like his maman, and she looked a bit like her too.

Lou was so hungry he would have eaten a cold rat. But Céline's hot soup was better.

Eighteen

Lou worked hard at practise all week. He wasn't going to take anything for granted, now that he knew the truth about girls' hockey. If he wanted to be the best, it wasn't going to happen just because he was a boy under his bloomers; it would only happen because of what he did with the puck.

Lou tried not to laugh out loud when he found out the name for those funny pants the team wore — bloomers. "Is that because they look like flowers?" he asked Claire. Because they did, like the ones that sprung open all around his house in spring.

"No," she said. "They were named after someone named Amelia Bloomer, who first starting wearing them in America."

The girls wore their bloomers when they played mid-week against the Flyers in Trois-Rivières, three hours away by train. Coach said all their games were on Saturdays, but this was an exception, since no one could buy tickets anyway. The public was actually not allowed to watch women's hockey in Trois-Rivières. Because of that, it was a quiet game. The only sounds were the sounds of the game: skates slashing the ice, pucks hitting sticks, and girls calling across the arena to each other, looking for passes or cheering each other on. But all around them was silence, like they were in church while everyone was praying.

Lou missed the rush the crowd noise had given him in the first game, but he tried not to let it bother him. He played better than the last game, and he and Claire and Bernadette were more precise with their passes. He picked up that Claire had a way of turning her head toward him and swinging out her left hip when she was going to pass him the puck, so he was ready. And when she wanted the puck, she tapped the ice three times with her stick. Bernadette and Claire could pass the puck right across center ice to each other, but Lou made sure he was always in the middle, ready for any opportunity. He scored once, on a pass from Claire, and she scored once on a pass from Bernadette.

"You're starting to play like a trio," Coach said at intermission. "Keep it up." But they couldn't score again. The Bakers' third goal came from Alice, the best of the McGill girls, leading the team to a 3–1 victory.

On the train ride home, Lou replayed his goal over and over in his mind. Even though there was no crowd to cheer, his whole team had erupted and that felt good.

He looked over at Alice and wondered if she felt the same way he did. The English girls were sitting across the aisle, talking away. Lou wondered what would happen if he were to go and sit with them. On the ice and on the bench they were one team, and they cheered each other's goals, but off the ice was another story altogether.

Saturday's game was against the second-best team, the Ottawa Alerts. Their best player was Eva Ault, although from what Lou had heard she wasn't nearly as good as Lapensée. Still, he wasn't taking any chances this time. He would be ready.

The Victoria Rink was as packed as it had been last Saturday. It was like this was the best entertainment in town, in spite of the fact that Lou had seen posters for concerts and dances on his Sunday walk. Nothing could compare to the excitement of hockey, even if it was only girls playing. Claire had told Lou that the five games they'd played without him had also been sold out, and Monsieur Robichaud had said that only the Canadiens, who played at the Montreal Arena, drew a bigger crowd.

"Don't forget what I promised, girls," Coach said as they skated in warm-up. "After three wins, we're off to see the Canadiens. If that doesn't make you move, I don't know what will. If you were boys I'd threaten to kick you in the pants!"

The girls didn't need a kick. Lou was getting to know them slowly, and each one had her reason for being here. Even if their reasons were different from his, they all shared two things in common: their love of hockey and the knowledge that this was their greatest chance at adventure. One girl, Simone, had even escaped from a convent to play. As the eldest girl, her parents had promised her to the nuns years ago, but after saying her goodbyes and boarding the eastbound train, she had gotten off at the next stop and waited for the next train back west.

"I ducked so low in my seat when we went past my town," Simone told them. "I had a feeling my parents would be checking the windows. They thought my little bag was full of bibles and rosaries, but all I had were my brother's old skates."

"My parents wanted me to marry an old man, just because he had money," said Marie-Claude, who played center on the second French line. "I said I'd rather die, and they told me not to blaspheme. So I told them I'd marry him if they let me come to Montreal to visit my aunt Josephine first, and they said okay. Well, my aunt let me stay, and she comes to all our games. You know the woman who shouts the loudest from the stands? Without her, I'd be barefoot and pregnant by now."

At every game, Marie-Claude's aunt cheered from the boardwalk. She had a horn with a big ball on the end that she squeezed to make even more noise whenever one of the Bakers had the puck. Madame Oliver said she was their number one fan.

"And you, Lou Lou. What's your story? Why are you here?" Magdalène asked him.

"Oh, it's not interesting," he replied, hanging his head.

"Lou Lou doesn't like to talk, girls," said Claire. Lately she had been coming to his rescue a lot, speaking for him and defending him. He was glad, but something about it made him uncomfortable too. He didn't know why she was doing it.

He longed to be able to tell his story. It was also full of deception and intrigue, just the sort of story the girls would like. But, of course, he couldn't. Besides, when he thought about their stories, he realized they were different from his in one big way. He had decided for himself to dress up as a girl in order to play in the big city, on the big rink. When he'd had enough, or when he'd beaten Lapensée, he could find a way out and go back to his old life. Then he could keep playing hockey and try to make it to the NHA, like he and Georges had always talked about. But for these girls, it was like somebody else had decided what they should do in life. Playing hockey was their own choice, but it was one they'd had to lie and cheat to make. And when it was all over, what could they go back to? The only ones with any choice at all were the few university girls on the team, and they were all English. Maybe Francine was right — he had stolen the spot of some girl from somewhere, maybe one just like Claire, when he'd joined the team.

Lou was sharp against the Alerts. Without Lapensée there to run him down like a steam engine he skated more freely and ended the night with one goal and two assists, one to Claire and one to Bernadette. Violet, another McGill girl, also scored once. Four goals for the Bakers. Coach was thrilled. Lou was happy, but he wished he had been able to score again. Then he would have tied Eva Ault, who had scored twice, the only goals for her team. She wasn't as good as Lapensée, but she was pretty close. Better than Lou had imagined.

Nineteen

ou played so well that the next morning, at breakfast, Madame Oliver read the girls an excerpt from *La Presse*, the daily paper:

THE MONTREAL BAKERS, owned by the Oliver family of the Oliver Bakery, have a new forward: Lou Lou Lapierre. She skates with finesse and can take the puck through traffic with incredible ease. She scored one goal and had two assists, leading them to a 4–2 victory, but she had many fine chances. Could the Montreal Westerns, long considered the number one women's hockey team in this city, finally have some serious competition?

The girls all clapped, and Lou felt himself blush, just like a real girl.

"Here," said Madame Oliver. "Save this and show it

to your parents when you go home at Christmas. They will be very proud."

Lou took the newspaper up to his room to look at the article again, in private. He hadn't wanted to gloat in front of the girls, but now he could. His first write-up; one of many, he hoped. One day, Papa and Monsieur Geoffrion would be reading news about him down at the train station, news that would spread through the town like the wildfires that sometimes ravaged the Gatineau hills in summer.

Lou lay on his bed and flipped through the rest of the newspaper. An article on the front page of the News section caught his eye: "Battle in Belgium Heating Up." Lou's mouth fell open. Georges was in Belgium. Until now, whenever he'd thought of Georges he'd pictured him bored to death down in his dark hole. But maybe that wasn't the case. He read on:

THE SECOND BATTLE OF PASSCHENDAELE, which ended three weeks ago, on November 10, 1917, has taken its toll on the Canadian Army, in particular the 1st and 2nd divisions, having taken over the front from the 3rd and 4th. The battle began in July and has been waged largely in a horrific sea of mud, from which our men, at least those who make it home, may never feel completely free. Casualties will certainly number in the tens of thousands, but the exact figure will not be known for years to come. No doubt mothers and fathers throughout Quebec, already angry that their sons may soon be forced to fight, will be mourning more bad news soon enough, if Prime Minister Borden has his way.

Lou choked back his tears. What would his parents care about him scoring goals and making perfect passes if Georges had been hurt, or worse? He couldn't say the terrible word. Before each game Monsieur Robichaud told them to get out there and kill their opponents, but he didn't really mean it. Not in that way.

For the second Sunday in a row, Lou pled sick and in need of a day of rest when Madame Oliver came to see if he would join them for their day of church and culture. He waited half an hour to be sure they'd be far from home, got dressed in his old clothes, and tiptoed downstairs. Once again he could hear Céline in the kitchen making their Sunday dinner. She wouldn't come looking for him. She was far too busy. He knew she was baking bread by the smell of warm yeast, and it made him think of home. For the first time since he'd arrived, he wished he was back in the kitchen with Maman, helping her roll out her dough. He didn't care what Papa thought about it. In fact, Madame Oliver had told them that all the head bakers at the Oliver Bakery were men. It was actually their profession. Papa would probably faint if he knew that.

But, as Lou was starting to realize, Papa didn't know much about the world outside their little town.

Twenty

L ou couldn't get down to the port fast enough. It was even busier than last week. Two men were standing on ladders, steadying a huge Christmas tree that was being erected in the middle of Place Jacques Cartier. From where Lou was standing it looked even taller than the statue of Lord Nelson. The windows and balconies of the hotels and restaurants were even more decorated, with big red ribbons and strings of lights that probably sparkled at night.

Lou was surprised by how pleased he was to see Boss down near the water again, this time throwing boxes onto the back of a horse-drawn wagon. "Well, if it isn't Lou," Boss said, smiling. "Here to make more money, are you? We could use a hand. I need someone to sit with the boxes and make sure they don't fall off when we go over the cobblestones. Jean here is a wild driver. We're off to Dupuis Frères. Are you up for it, little man?"

Lou nodded. It felt good to be called a man, even if

he was little. Maybe he'd make another twenty cents. He squeezed himself between the boxes, holding out his arms to create a barrier as the horse slowly turned around and headed off along rue de la Commune, then up Saint-Denis to Sainte-Catherine. So many streets and so many stores! You could take all the buildings in the valley and string them together and they wouldn't equal one of these Montreal streets. When the horse clopped past a tavern, Lou wondered if the bad stuff Father Béliveau had warned them about was hiding in there. At least, it must have been hiding, because from the outside the city didn't look very sinful. Of course it was Sunday, and most everything was closed.

Was Boss sure this Dupuis Frères would be open? He might not get paid if it wasn't. Lou had no idea where the store was, but if it made him more money and got him away from the girls for a few hours, he was all for it. There were times when Lou found it so hard pretending to be a girl that he wanted to scream. He'd lock himself in the bathroom for an hour, pretending to bathe, just to sit and be himself. He wasn't sure how much longer he could do it, but it would be a shame to go home without beating Lapensée. Working would also take his mind off that horrible article in the newspaper, the one about Belgium.

Half an hour later they reached a huge store that took up a whole block. A row of windows showed stacks and stacks of goods: stuff for kitchens and bathrooms, toys and tools. Mannequins wore fancy Christmas dresses, short enough to show their ankles, with fur ruffles around their necks. He thought of Francine and what she would say, looking at all the nice things. Lou knew that she'd never had a new dress, not with three older sisters. By the time they came to her they were always tattered. He could see her in that red one with the gray lace.

A sign on the front door said, "Closed/Fermé." The wagon turned the corner and came to a stop beside a large steel door at the side of the store.

"You, little man," Boss shouted. "Start unloading." Jean reached up and grabbed the boxes from Lou and stacked them on the sidewalk. Two workers, who looked about the same age as Georges, opened the large doors from inside the store. They barely looked up at the boss or Jean or Lou and continued talking as though no one else was around.

"I like the one with the blond hair, the fast skater. I'd like to see her move across something other than ice," one of them said.

"Yeah, like what, Jacques?" the other one shouted as he winched open the door.

"Like me," Jacques replied, and they both laughed.

"Or the goalie? They say she's related to Vézina. Do you think it's true? She's way prettier than him."

Lou's breath caught in his throat. They were talking about the Bakers. The one with the blond hair must be

Claire. What would she say if he repeated what Jacques had said about her? When the other girls talked about boys, she got very quiet. Once she had told them that she would never marry, which had made them laugh, like she was telling a joke. Claire had stamped her foot and said she was serious, which put an end to the laughter.

"That little one is kind of cute too, and fast!" The guy winked and winked, like he had a sudden twitch. "And she knows how to score." This set Jacques laughing and swaying his hips.

Lou froze. That was him they were complimenting. And the way the guy was winking, Lou knew he was talking about more than hockey. He felt his face turn red. He wanted to jump off the wagon and punch the guy right in the face for talking about him that way. Papa was right. It was hard being a girl.

"Lapenseé knows how to score too, but you can have her ... or him, if the rumors are true," said Jacques.

"Hey, are you helping or not?" shouted Boss. Lou realized he was standing there, immobile, doing nothing. The idea of rumors about Lapensée being a boy scared him; what if he scored too many goals and people starting thinking the same of him? Except Lapensée was so much bigger. It was easier to think she was a guy.

"And you boys, get your minds out of the gutter," Boss called over to the two store employees. "Don't just stand there like a couple of girls."

All this talk about girls had Lou flustered. He almost dropped a box, throwing it out before Jean was ready.

"Hey, watch the merchandise, little man," called Boss.

When all the boxes were unloaded, Lou asked if he could ride as far west along Sainte-Catherine as they were going. He had to get back. Last week, Madame Oliver and the girls had come home just after one o'clock, and he assumed they'd do the same today.

He didn't even feel that excited when Boss handed him a quarter, even though it was the first one he'd ever owned. His head was heavy with thoughts of Georges and of all the things he'd had to keep to himself today. It suddenly seemed too hard. What if he just ran away from Madame Oliver's and tried to get a job working for Boss? He could get word to Maman somehow. As long as he was safe and making money she wouldn't mind. He could be a boy all the time, and he could still play hockey for fun. Sooner or later someone from a big team would notice him.

But then he remembered the sound of the cheers that ripped through the crowd when he scored. And the article in the paper today. He would miss all that, even though all he'd had was a taste. He wanted more of it, and right now this was the only way to get it.

He added the quarter to his two dimes, deep under his mattress, and changed back into his girls' clothes, hoping he didn't smell too much like horse.

Twenty-One

There were only two more games until the Christmas break, when Lou would get to go home. It was the game against the Vics that he was most anxious about, his chance to beat Lapensée. It had been two weeks since the Bakers had played them, and he knew he had developed a lot of skill in that time. How Lou wished his parents could watch him play, and Georges. Every day Lou took Madame Oliver's copy of *La Presse* upstairs to his room and looked for more news on the war. He had written to his parents and begged them to call from the station if there was anything they needed to tell him. Madame Oliver had a phone on the wall in the hallway. Every time it rang, Lou's heart jumped. What if it was Papa with terrible news?

On Saturday, a few hours before the game, Madame Oliver announced there would be a special treat for the team. They were to have a tour of the Oliver Bakery. They met at the large red-brick building, and Monsieur

Oliver, Madame Oliver's brother, shook each of their hands. When he got to Lou, he stopped and said, "Ah, yes, the little speedboat. I've seen you play, but now I'm very happy to meet you." Like his sister, Monsieur Oliver spoke perfect French, but with a heavy English accent.

Lou would have preferred to be compared to a locomotive rather than a speedboat, but he smiled anyway.

Monsieur Oliver showed them the huge steel vats where batter was mixed by electric mixers, the long wall of ovens where the bread baked, and the row of tables where workers in white hats gathered rolls and loaves and put them in boxes. Lou thought of Maman at home, making up to six loaves of her famous molasses bread at a time. What would she say about all this? The factory was impressive, but Maman's kitchen smelled so much better. And there were no spoons to lick here. Still, Monsieur Oliver allowed each of the girls to take a couple of treats. Lou took a sticky bun with raisins and a roll filled with jam.

"Fuel for tonight, girls," said Monsieur Oliver. "To beat Lapensée." At the mention of her name, a murmur of boos whipped around the room.

They went straight from the bakery to the rink to warm up and get ready for the game.

The arena was more packed than usual because of Lapensée. She had her own cheering section behind the Vics' net. Her fans chanted her name, drawing out its three syllables, "La-pen-sée," and adding, "Hey hey

hey" at the end. Each "hey" was louder than the last. Obviously Lapensée's fans didn't care about any rumors. If only Lou's reputation was big enough for him to have his own cheering section and his own chant. He could hear it in his head. "Lo-co-Lou — voo, voo, voo." Maybe after this game, that would happen.

At center ice, Lou was still overwhelmed by Lapensée's size and by the way she glared into his eyes, a confident smirk on her face. He remembered how she had run him over last time, so he dug in his blades, ready to fly. When the referee dropped the puck for the opening faceoff he darted to the side, taking the puck with him. He could hear Lapensée grunt behind him. The sound followed him all the way up the rink and broke off only when he passed the puck to Claire. She skated parallel to him toward the net then passed it back. Lou darted between the defense, hit the puck, and scored.

It was the first time all year that Lapensée had not scored the first goal of a game. Her cheering section let out a chorus of boos that floated up through the wooden rafters, but all around the rink the cheers grew even louder. Marie-Claude's aunt had found more horns, and she had a whole crew of women with her, honking horns and cheering like a flock of crazy geese.

Lou glanced their way as he skated to the bench. They were leaning so far into the rink their fingers grazed his sweater. Then, up ahead, Lou spotted two familiar faces. They too were leaning into the ice, cheering. His feet turned to blocks of wood as he recognized the guys from Dupuis Frères, the store workers. They must come to all the games. That's how they knew the players so well. Lou was going to have to skate right past them. He remembered what they had said about him scoring, how that had made them wink, and he knew they weren't talking about hockey. He hung his head as low as he could, even though that wasn't what a champion should do. Someone who just scored a goal should be skating with his head high, letting the whole arena see his smile.

But he couldn't take that chance.

He felt their breath in his ears as they yelled when he skated past, so close they could have plucked the tuque off his head. He rested on the bench for a minute, until coach was poking him to get back out there. He worked as hard as he could to forget that Jacques and his friend were there. But wherever he skated, he could feel them watching. He tried to block out the entire arena — cheers, boos, and all — and just focus on the puck. He reminded himself that those guys had barely looked his way on Sunday, and he had been up on the wagon anyway. Plus, with the red tuque covering half his face, there was no way they could know him.

But it was no use. His game was suffering. He hadn't been back out twenty seconds when Lapensée grabbed the puck from his stick and zoomed toward Magdalène.

She twisted and turned and flung herself at the puck, but she couldn't stop Lapensée's shot. The game was now tied. All because of Lou.

He couldn't let this happen. Not against the Vics. Beating this Miracle Maid was why he'd tried out for the team in the first place, why he was going through the torture of wearing girls' clothes. Then he remembered the two guys at Dupuis Frères joking about Lapensée being a boy. What if the rumor got so big the league decided to test everyone, breasts or not? After all, those could be faked too. Lou would have to play as though every game might be his last.

At the next faceoff, Lou jumped on the puck and took off. All around him, a chant started up, low at first, then gaining momentum. The chant rose as he neared the Vics' net. "Lou Lou Lou." It spurred him on. He pulled back as though he were going to shoot, then he dipped left and gently slipped the puck between the goalie's legs. She was caught completely off guard. She smashed her stick against the ice and cracked it in half. Lou knew that was exactly the type of gesture that kept Father Béliveau from letting them have a girls' team at home. That and the stream of curses that escaped her mouth.

Horns and cheers accompanied Lou back to center ice. Lapensée loomed above him in the faceoff circle. He was sure she'd added bulk since the game started, but he reminded himself that even if she had size, he had speed. Still, without the puck, speed was nothing. Lapensée bulldozed him to the ground, flew to the net, and scored her second goal of the game. The first period ended in a 2–2 tie.

"Best period ever, girls," Coach Robichaud said. "It's the closest we've ever been to the Vics. Keep it going."

Somehow, the whole team played better in the second period. Danielle was a stone wall whenever the Vics tried to get past her. Even Lapensée had no choice but to scrape along the boards with little space to move. Lou made two perfect passes, one to Bernadette and one to Claire, each resulting in a goal. But Lapensée matched both with goals of her own. It was like each Baker goal made her fiercer and more determined. The second period ended tied again, 4–4. In the third period everyone slowed down. They had nothing left. Lou's legs felt soft as a rag doll's, like the one Francine's baby sister carted around wherever she went. Lapensée didn't score again either, even though she had several chances. Magdalène played the game of her life in front of the net, keeping the game at a tie.

The final score was 4–4. The Bakers had tied the mighty Vics. And for once Lou had scored more than one goal in a game.

The Bakers' bench erupted when the final whistle blew. The girls gathered around Lou, lifted him up in the air, and skated him around. The arena was still chanting his name, "Lou Lou Lou." It was like he was in a dream.

In a minute he'd wake up and Maman would be shouting at him to chop some more wood for the stove.

Across the rink the Vics were also huddled, but in a different way. The girls were holding Lapensée back. From atop the girls' shoulders, Lou could see her straining to break loose. He knew what she wanted to do. She wanted to skate over to him and smash her stick over his head. He'd wanted to do the same to her the last time they'd played.

In the dressing room the cheers continued as Lou grabbed his clothes and headed to the washroom to change. He had to do it fast. A sports writer from *La Presse* was waiting for him. Suddenly Claire was banging on the door.

"Hurry up, Lou Lou. He won't wait forever."

"I'm coming," Lou replied. He dreaded this interview. Monsieur Geoffrion, the station master, might read it. How could he answer questions without giving away who he was?

"Coach said I should go with you," said Claire. She took his hand and practically pulled him down the boardwalk to where the man was sitting, a pad and pencil in his hand. Lou would have sat further away, but Claire sat next to him and shoved him over so that his knees were almost touching the reporter's.

"Let's get right to it. I'm Philippe Savard. And you, Lou Lou Lapierre, are a great player. Where did you learn to play hockey?"

"On the lake at home," said Lou.

"Like all kids in Quebec," said Monsieur Savard. "But where exactly?"

He'd have to say it. Coach knew the name of his town. "Saint-Christophe."

"And did you have older brothers to show you the game?"

"Yes, I have an older brother. But in my town, all the kids play, boys and girls." It was sort of true, except the girls weren't in teams. It was just for fun, after the real games, when the boys would finally let them on the ice and lend them their sticks.

"And who motivates you? Who is your idol?"

"I am a big fan of Didier Pitre."

"But he's a man. It must be hard to find idols as a female player."

Lou just shrugged. This was the first interview of his life. He should be talking up a storm. But he just wanted it to be over.

"And what are your plans for the future?"

"Well, I want to play in the —" Lou stopped short, just in time. He couldn't say that he wanted to play in the NHA. He had to say something else — something a girl could say. But what *could* a girl say to that question?

"I just want to play hockey," he said, shrugging again. Monsieur Savard would think he was simple-minded, like the coach had thought Papa was that day at the house.

"Lou Lou is very shy. She doesn't like to talk about herself," Claire jumped in. "But we all know she's going to keep playing for many years and maybe help change the rules so that more girls can play hockey."

Monsieur Savard smiled. That was the type of answer he was looking for.

"And your name is?"

"Claire Doucette, right wing. I scored tonight too."

"That's right, you did, and you played a wonderful game as well." Monsieur Savard turned back to Lou. "And what's your real name?" Lou's heart stopped. What did the reporter mean? Did he know something?

"I mean, Lou Lou must be short for Louise, right?"

Lou nodded. So far, it was his only outright lie.

Then a photographer appeared, carrying a big camera with a flash bulb. "Move closer together," he instructed Claire and Lou. Claire obliged, pushing right up against Lou and putting her arm around him. She was squeezing him so tightly it hurt.

Lou dipped his head down as far as he could without disappearing altogether. Even if Monsieur Geoffrion didn't care to read an article about girls playing hockey, he'd look at the picture. No man could resist peeking at a pretty girl like Claire.

Twenty-Two

Monsieur Oliver had bought the team first-class tickets to Ottawa, where they would play their last game before the Christmas break. Unlike when they'd played in Trois-Rivières, where they had left in the morning and come back at night, this time they would stay at a hotel in Ottawa before going home the next morning. What would Maman say if she knew Lou was going to stay in an actual hotel? And what would Father Béliveau say? He slipped the word "hotel" into a lot of his sermons when he was talking about the sins of the big city. Would Lou see those sins first-hand Saturday night?

Everyone was dizzy with excitement over the road trip. Well, everyone except Lou. He didn't want to spend the night away from Madame Oliver's, where he had his routine all worked out. No one bothered him anymore about the way he locked the bathroom door or only changed when he was alone. They had even left him alone again on Sunday.

"Perhaps Lou Lou needs a day to herself once in a while," he'd heard Madame Oliver tell the other girls. "Although I will have to tell her parents she isn't attending church. I'll let them decide if that's a problem or not. After all, we did promise your parents and guardians you'd go to church every Sunday."

He'd made another quarter, this time helping Boss organize his shed at the port. It was just him, Boss, and Jean, and they'd worked without speaking, which suited Lou fine. He was glad they weren't going back to Dupuis Frères, although part of him wanted to hear what the boys would have to say about the Bakers' impressive tie with the Vics. That picture of him and Claire had been center of the sports page, with the article underneath. Monsieur Savard had added some words, so Lou came off sounding smarter than he had in real life. The reporter had even written that women's hockey was getting to be every bit as entertaining as men's. And he'd bestowed a new nickname on Lou: "Lightning Lou Lou." Maybe that was better than "Locomotive." After all, sometimes those chugged along pretty slowly. But lightning! It was the most powerful force in nature. Lou had a distinct memory of Papa and Georges going out with saws and axes to cut down huge trees that had been split down the middle by lightning during a storm. Lou could split the defense the same way, in a flash.

Sitting on the train, Lou worried about the night at the hotel. They were going to be four to a room, so all of

Madame Oliver's charges were staying together, two to a bed. Sleeping across the room from Claire was one thing, but being in the same bed was another. He'd have to find a way to curl up against the wall and avoid turning over, all night long.

"My God, Lou Lou. What's with you?" asked Bernadette. "You're all red in the face."

"Are you sick?" asked Danielle.

Claire stared at him calmly. "She's probably just excited. Right, Lou?" She had taken to calling him Lou, which he didn't like. Every time she said it, he felt a jolt. He kept his eyes down because he knew she would be gazing at him intently.

"Sure, I just don't like bridges," he said. Luckily the train was clanking over the big iron bridge that crossed the Lake of Two Mountains.

"Oh, Lou Lou. You're a funny girl. You're so brave out on the ice and such a chicken everywhere else," said Bernadette.

"But we still love you, of course," added Danielle. Lou hoped this wouldn't lead to one of those group hugs the girls loved so much.

"Oh, Lou Lou. Scared of a bridge?" Claire said suddenly, standing up. Marie-Claude's aunt, who was chaperoning them as well, put down her knitting to listen to Claire.

"Girls, Lou Lou thought the bridge was going to collapse," Claire announced. A chorus of *ahs* rose up around him from all sides. The girls ran up to him one at a time and hugged him, telling him they understood. Even the McGill girls had a turn.

Lou shrunk inside the huddle. The thoughts in his head swirled around, more violently than the water in the choppy lake. Maybe he could escape in the Ottawa train station and hop on the Wakefield train and just go home. He closed his eyes and pictured Saint-Christophe as it would look from the train if he could find the nerve to run away. Would Francine be outside at this hour, or was she inside, peeling potatoes for the potage that would cook slowly all day over the fire? And was Maman feeding the chickens? He could see the lake and his house just beyond it, the black roof hidden behind a cluster of maple trees, a puff of smoke rising from the chimney. Or maybe Maman was in the kitchen, baking. He could jump off the train and run home to help her. Anything would be better than spending a night in a hotel room with Claire, hiding who he really was.

He'd already lasted longer than he'd planned, and he'd come close to beating Lapensée last week. Shouldn't that be enough?

"Okay, girls. Let's give Lou Lou some space," Claire said finally, pushing everyone away. She was a funny one. She'd pulled them all over in the first place. Now she was sending them away. Not for the first time, Lou noticed how Claire liked to put herself in charge. Maybe she'd learned that at the orphanage. She was the eldest and had been living there the longest. Lou supposed that gave her some sort of authority over the other girls.

He turned his face to the window and spent the rest of the ride watching snow-covered fields whip past and counting the cows that huddled for shelter under trees.

Twenty-Three

The Ottawa Arena was not as fancy as the Victoria Rink, but it was packed with fans cheering on the Alerts. Eva Ault was a different player on home ice. She challenged Lou at every chance, and he could tell that the Alerts' coach was deliberately matching them up. Every time Lou stepped on the ice, Ault did too. They stood across from each other at faceoffs, practically the same height, their sticks tapping the ice in anticipation.

Apart from Ault, the Alerts were weak on offense, but their defense was strong. He would never say this to Danielle, but it was stronger than the Bakers'. Again and again Lou felt their force as they knocked him over and tripped him with their skates. Their feet were big, like men's. His only chance was to skate fast and deke around them. He reminded himself that he was now Lightning Lou, a blazing streak that could cut through anything. But he simply couldn't play his best, not with the thought of spending the night in a hotel room sitting heavily on his mind. He tried to forget about it and focus on the Alerts' net, but every now and then the thought of sleeping in the same bed as Claire would hit him and almost knock him over, as forcefully as the Alerts' defense.

Ault ended up outscoring him again. She had four goals by the end of the game. Lou only had two. Claire and Alice each had one, so the Alerts and Bakers ended the night in a tie, four to four, just like the Bakers' last game.

"Tying the Vics is one thing, girls," Coach Robichaud said. "But the Alerts? You had them beat last time. We need to go forward, not backward, right?" He looked around and waited until every girl had nodded her head. Lou nodded too. The coach was right. He should have played better. The team would never progress if he didn't, if they all didn't.

After they'd washed and changed, the girls climbed into several waiting taxicabs and headed to the hotel. Some of them literally screamed when they saw the Château Laurier, which rose up beside the Ottawa River like a castle, with tall towers and green turrets. Lou had never seen such a luxurious building in his entire life, and he wished he could telephone Maman right away and tell her about it.

Madame Oliver and Marie-Claude's aunt Josephine ushered them into the dining room, where they took up five round tables covered in white cloths. A waiter in a black suit and bow tie poured water into their glasses from silver pitchers. Each plate was surrounded by two spoons, two knives, and two forks. Lou wondered if they'd made a mistake when setting the table, but didn't dare ask. The girls sat perfectly still while the waiter hovered, but burst out laughing after he left.

"Decorum, girls," Madame Oliver reminded them, tapping the table with a silver teaspoon.

The butter was shaped like seashells. Who had done that? Lou pictured a woman who looked like Maman in the kitchen, doing nothing but sculpting butter.

"This is the finest hotel in the country. It's where lords and ladies stay," Madame Oliver said. "You are very lucky girls. My brother is a fine businessman. When he opens his new bakery in Ottawa, he's going to supply this hotel for a very good price. That's how we got the deal on your rooms. Do you think the Vics stay at this hotel when they play here?"

Dinner was the juiciest roast beef Lou had ever tasted, with roasted potatoes and creamy cucumber salad. For dessert they ate crème caramel, with burnt crust on top that cracked and splintered like ice on the lake when Lou dug in his spoon. Each bite was such a delight that Lou almost forgot his fear, until Madame Oliver said, "All right, girls, enough food for one night. Now to bed."

The meal roiled in Lou's stomach, and he prayed it wouldn't come up. Claire, Bernadette, and Danielle linked arms as they stood jiggling in the elevator. When the attendant, who wore a bright red jacket, closed the golden gate, Lou imagined it was the gate of a prison cell, one where they locked up fraudsters like him. And maybe Lapensée, too, if the rumors were true.

"This one is yours," Madame Oliver said, pointing to a door. "Now, don't stay up late. I'll be back in an hour to check that you're all in bed and quiet."

The three girls ran inside while Lou stood in the doorway and took in the room. It was impressive. There were two high beds, with massive headboards sculpted into leaves at the top. The bedspreads were dark red with gold tassels, the same material as the curtains. There were heavy wood bureaus and tables with mirrors and velvet seats. A thick white carpet lay on the floor, so deep Lou's feet sunk into it. He wished he could sink in completely, like in a deep snowdrift. The girls were already pulling off their clothes, stripping down to their underwear and jumping on the beds. He didn't know where to look.

"Come on, Lou, it's fun," said Claire. "No one can see us. We don't have to be perfect little ladies in here. It's fantastic. It reminds me of home, when the nuns would finally say goodnight and leave us alone."

"In a minute," he said, grabbing his nightgown and heading for the bathroom.

"Oh no, not tonight," said Claire. "Girls, let's get her."

The three girls jumped off the bed and ran toward Lou.

He froze. The bathroom was only a few feet away, but it seemed like miles. This was all way too much. Why hadn't he run away at the station when he'd had the chance? He'd even seen the sign for the Wakefield train, leaving in twenty minutes. His brain floated over all the advice Francine had given him. How to join in. How to eat. How to laugh. How to pretend to be shocked. Maybe that was the one to use now.

He screamed and ran to the bathroom. Its lit doorway was like the net and he was the puck, darting straight for it as fast as he could. He quickly locked the door behind him. Bernadette, Danielle, and Claire pounded on it, trying to get him to open up.

"I'm taking a bath," he called over their pounding. He could hear them groan. This tub was even deeper than Madame Oliver's, and the towels were as thick as four of his towels at home, the ones Maman ordered from the Eaton's catalogue. He knew it was luxury, pure luxury. But all he could feel was misery.

After a while, the girls stopped pounding and protesting, and it actually grew quiet in the room. Lou couldn't stay in the water forever. His skin was puckered like a raisin. He dried off and pulled on the flannel nightgown and underclothes that hid his body. When he came out the girls were all huddled on one bed, reading a *Life* magazine that had a picture of a woman in a flowing white gown on the cover. She was holding up a torch. Behind her, a group of soldiers were gathered. The words "For Liberty" were written underneath. It reminded Lou that his problems were small compared to Georges's. God knew where he was now or what he was doing, but Lou was sure Georges would trade places with him in a flash. Who wouldn't rather be in a fancy hotel room with three pretty girls than down in a muddy trench?

Lou climbed into bed and rolled close to the wall. He needed to say something. Things would get hard fast if these three girls, who had been so kind to him, turned against him.

"I'm sorry, girls. I didn't want to be mean, not playing with you. I'm just not in a playful mood. I'm feeling homesick, being so close to home again."

That was all they needed to hear. They grabbed their pillows and surrounded him, pounding him playfully. He turned into a ball and waited for the storm to pass.

When they'd spent all their energy, the girls slid under the covers. Danielle and Bernadette called goodnight from across the room. Claire and Lou called it back. Lou imagined their voices clashing somewhere on the high ceiling, near the fancy plasterwork around the chandelier. Then he closed his eyes and prayed Claire would leave him alone.

A few seconds later, Madame Oliver entered the room. She must have had her own key. "Ah, wonderful girls. You're all in bed. And so quiet! I must say I'm surprised. Sleep well."

Lou held his limbs tight. Claire had told him that it was after the nuns' final inspection that the girls in her orphanage really cut loose. Would she take Madame Oliver's departure as some sort of signal?

Suddenly he felt a hand on his head — Claire's, stroking his long hair down to his shoulder. "When the new girls were sad, this is what we'd do," he heard her whisper. "Do you like it?"

Lou wanted to shout no, but he couldn't. The truth was, it did feel good. Too good. His whole body was starting to squirm.

"Okay, goodnight, sweet Lou Lou," Claire said. She rolled toward him and kissed the top of his head.

Mon dieu, thought Lou.

Twenty-Four

M onsieur Oliver himself showed up at the arena during practise on Wednesday to congratulate the team on their success. Their record for the season, including the games that had been played before Lou arrived, was five wins, four losses, and two ties, which put them in second place, behind the Vics but ahead of the Alerts. The fourth-place team was the Montreal Westerns, the other Montreal team. The Bakers had played them twice before Lou arrived and had lost both times. But they were struggling now and had slipped to fourth. The Trois-Rivières Flyers, maybe because of the quietness of their arena, were dead last.

"You are moving up, girls, I have no doubt, and you have made the entire bakery very proud. You are becoming the pride of Montreal, in fact," he said. "And I wish to reward you for it." He pulled an envelope out of his jacket pocket and waved it in the air. "In here, my dears, are tickets for the game tomorrow night at the

Montreal Arena. You will see the Montreal Canadiens take on their archrivals, the Toronto Blueshirts."

All around Lou, the girls jumped up and down. He bounced a little so he'd blend in, but what he really wanted to do was pump his fist in the air and shout, "Hooray!" at the top of his lungs. Coach had said they needed three wins before going to see the Canadiens, but two wins and two ties had done it. Maybe Monsieur Oliver counted the tie against the formidable Vics as a win, since it was the closest any other team had come.

"Of course, my sister and I, and Coach Robichaud, will be there too. Now, practice hard, girls. I want more victories. My sales skyrocket with every one of your wins, you know."

As Lou skated, he composed a letter home in his head. He wouldn't make it too braggy, especially since Francine would be the one reading it to Maman and Papa. *The most incredible thing in the world is happening to me tomorrow.* No. *Tomorrow I am doing something really exciting.* No. *Tomorrow the whole team is going to watch the Canadiens play.*

Never mind! He'd just tell them about it in a few days when he was back home. And he'd write it in the letter Maman was going to ask him to write to Georges. Georges was going to be so jealous, but still he'd want to know. Lou decided he would describe the game in detail, to give Georges something to take his mind off the mud and the gas and the enemies.

"Wear your own skirts or dresses, but put the uniform sweater on top and wear the tuque," said Madame Oliver after dinner the next day. "We want people to know who you are. You heard my brother. People are starting to take notice. You'll be as famous as the Canadiens soon enough."

Lou was glad. Dressing was always tough. The only thing he really felt comfortable in was the Bakers' uniform. He had taken to wearing the sweater on off days too, as soon as it was clean. The girls and Madame Oliver just added it to their list of ways in which he was different, but he could live with that.

Madame Oliver decided they should walk to the arena, which was only a few blocks west. It was a fresh December night, not too cold, with a light snow falling. The girls formed a line along Sherbrooke Street, two by two. Claire hooked her arm immediately into Lou's. She was as excited as he was.

"Tonight I will say an extra prayer for Sister Clothilde," said Claire as they passed the elegant gray stone buildings. "If it wasn't for her I wouldn't be here right now, walking with you to see a real live Canadiens hockey game."

"Really?" asked Lou.

"Oh yes, really. She had to pull lots of strings to let me come here for the year, believe me."

"For the year? What do you mean?"

"I've been given one year, to sow my wild oats, as

they say. Get it all out of my system. Then, when I get back, I will take my vows. Didn't you know?"

Lou shook his head. He didn't know what to say. He hadn't met many nuns, but the few he had met didn't seem like Claire. "But what if you want to keep playing?"

"Can't. Absolutely not. I'd have nowhere to live, no one to stay with. Sooner or later even Madame Oliver would want me to leave. And then what?"

"You could get married." Lou thought of Jacques. He knew there were more young men like him who'd love the chance to court Claire.

"No, Lou. That won't happen for me."

Lou stopped walking and turned to Claire. He wanted to tell her that she was one of the prettiest girls he'd ever seen, besides Francine. That he should know because he was a boy and boys knew what pretty girls looked like. But of course he couldn't. All he could do was say, "Why not?"

Claire's face turned red, and she pulled up her scarf to hide her cheeks. Lou had never seen Claire blush.

"Never mind. Just take my word for it. It's something I've always known, since I was little. Besides, what husband would let his wife play hockey?"

She was right. Imagine the men from Saint-Christophe allowing their wives to come to Montreal to play hockey. It would never happen.

They walked the rest of the way in silence, except for when Claire stopped to point out a squirrel in a tree or a cat in a window. Everything that moved caught her eye and delighted her. The thought of Claire living the rest of her life in a convent, possibly in complete silence, saddened Lou. No wonder Claire put so much into her play. She was squeezing an entire lifetime of action into one year.

Twenty-Five

The Montreal Arena was a marvel. Rows and rows of benches surrounded the ice. The girls had seats in the fifth row, and Monsieur Oliver had rented them rugs to sit on to keep their bottoms warm. Lou couldn't stop looking around. There were more people here than he'd ever seen in his life. Thousands, probably. Groups of fans were also gathered around the top, past the benches. The crowd erupted into a loud chorus of cheers when the Canadiens flew onto the ice.

Lou couldn't believe it. There, below him, in the flesh, was Newsy Lalonde, Papa's favorite player. Beside him skated Didier Pitre, Louis Berlinquette, Bert Corbeau, and Joe Malone, the Phantom. An announcer stood on a tall wooden box and called the players' names into a large horn as they jumped onto the ice, but the sound was drowned out by the crowd. Good thing Lou knew their numbers. Bad Joe Hall was as big as he'd expected, his back as broad as a wagon. Georges Vézina came out last, and the crowd cheered even louder. Lou could feel the bench vibrate beneath him.

The Blueshirts came out next. The crowd hissed and booed wildly. Lou realized his fists were in the air and he was stamping his feet. He almost stopped, but when he looked beside him he saw that all the girls were doing the same. So much for what Madame Oliver had told them about decorum.

When the referee held the puck over center ice, the crowd grew completely quiet, like everyone had sucked in their breath at the exact same second. They released it as the puck hit the ice. The game was non-stop action as the five players on each team skated from end to end. Lou grew dizzy following the puck. He loved the sound of the blades slicing the ice, skidding and spraying. When a Blueshirt came near Bad Joe Hall, he rounded out his chest and bounced the player into the boards. The crowd cheered, and Lou imagined the purple bruise that must already be sprouting on the Toronto player's chest. Newsy Lalonde skated so fast it was embarrassing to think how much faster Lou would have to get to make it to the NHA. He almost turned to Claire to tell her that, but then remembered he couldn't.

No one could know that it was his goal in life to one day be down there, playing on this team.

At intermission, Madame Oliver allowed them to buy lemonade at the concession stand. People pointed at their sweaters and said, "Hey, it's the ladies' team."

Some cheered, and others laughed. Lou wished he could puff himself up to Bad Joe Hall's size and ram the laughers into the wall. But, of course, he couldn't. Even if he really were a girl, he'd have to take it and smile.

By the end of the second period, the score was 4–2 for Montreal.

Danielle was begging Madame Oliver to be allowed back to the concession stand for ice cream when a loud voice boomed through the crowd. It was the man on the box again.

"Ladies and gentlemen," he called out. "As you may have noticed, we have special guests in the arena tonight." Lou and the girls looked all around to see whom he meant. "Our own Montreal Bakers, the fine ladies' hockey team, are in the house." Suddenly all eyes turned toward the bench where the Bakers were seated. "Hey, ladies," continued the announcer. "Come on down. Some people would like to meet you."

All of a sudden, Georges Vézina and Newsy Lalonde were skating back to center ice. Monsieur and Madame Oliver were waving the girls down the stairs. Could this really be happening? Lou felt like he was floating. Before he knew it, he was on the rink with the rest of the team, and Vézina and Lalonde were shaking the girls' hands. Magdalène and Vézina actually hugged, and for the first time Lou believed they were related. When Newsy Lalonde reached for him, Lou's knees caved in. Lalonde shook Lou's hand vigorously, then leaned down and whispered in his ear, "Too bad you're a girl. You'd have a future in this game."

Lou wanted to tear off his tuque and shout that he wasn't a girl. He was a boy, and he *would* play for the team one day. He wanted to beg Lalonde to let him try out now, but that was crazy. He'd need to wait at least five years before that could happen. In the meantime, if anyone found out he was a boy his career would be ruined. What team would want a player who had once worn a skirt?

He watched the other girls curtsy and bow their heads as the stars shook their hands. He had no choice. For now, he had to do the same.

Twenty-Six

Claire was the only one staying behind at Madame Oliver's for Christmas. "Are you sure you don't want to go home?" Danielle asked her. She and Bernadette had one arm each hooked around Claire's shoulders. Their bags were packed and waiting beside them in the hallway.

"No, I'd rather stay here. At least there are things to do in the city, if Madame Oliver will let me do them."

"But what about Sister Clothilde?" asked Bernadette.

"She's had me every Christmas for sixteen years, and she'll have me for many more, so no, I don't want to go home. I'll be fine, girls. Trust me."

The girls hugged and kissed. Lou allowed himself to be hugged by Claire, but he pulled away before she could kiss him.

At the station, the few girls who were taking trains hugged again and parted. Marie-Claude's aunt was chaperoning the girls boarding the eastbound trains toward Quebec City. Madame Oliver waited with Lou for the Ottawa train. Lou had everything he needed to change back into a boy in his bag, carefully hidden under his shirts.

"Have a merry Christmas, Lou Lou. Don't forget to give your parents the money."

"I won't."

"You're a wonderful daughter, Lou Lou. Your family will love those gifts."

He nodded. Yesterday he'd talked Madame Oliver into allowing the girls to visit Dupuis Frères. With the seventy cents he had saved working for the boss, he'd bought a sparkling star ornament for Maman, a green velvet hair ribbon for Francine, and a tin of hand cream for Papa. The cover said it was a miracle cure for cuts and burns.

Lou took a seat in the window, his dark coat pulled tight around him, and waved at Madame Oliver. He wished she'd leave already. What could possibly happen to him between now and the train pulling out? A group of young women wearing the long white veils of nurses were boarding the train. The porter was helping them load their large bags into the car. The wheels finally started turning, so he gave Madame Oliver a final wave. The second she was out of sight, he ran to the washroom and swapped the skirt for his old pants. He tucked his hair, which had grown past his shoulders, deep inside his tuque. He didn't want any remnant of

Lou Lou to show. Then he sat somewhere different so no one would notice how he'd changed. The nurses were loud, talking excitedly about their trip. They were off to Britain, to serve in the war. Lou couldn't help wonder what Father Béliveau would say.

Maman and Papa were at the station to meet him. Lou could see the relief on Papa's face when he walked off the train wearing his pants. Did Papa think that he was going to be a girl forever now? Maman hugged him so hard he couldn't breathe.

"Let the boy get some air, for heaven's sake," said Papa. "Here, son, give me your bag."

"Well, well, how was the bakery?" asked Monsieur Geoffrion, stepping out of his office. He gave a subtle wink to Papa, and Lou knew that his father must have confided in the station master. Papa just looked down at the rough boards of the station platform. It was clear he had only confessed because he'd had to. It must have been the article and photo in *La Presse*.

"The bakery is amazing," Lou said. "Very modern. There are ovens that reach all the way up to the ceiling and bake fifty loaves at a time." He was relieved that he didn't have to lie about that.

As they turned to leave, Monsieur Geoffrion waved him over. He bent down and whispered, so that only Lou could hear, "Hey, I read that the Bakers' new player is doing very well, that little Lightning Lou Lou is becoming something of a star in the city."

Lou smiled. He'd have to trust that Monsieur Geoffrion wouldn't betray him. Papa always said the station master could be trusted with anything. He wasn't the type to spread gossip. If he did, he'd lose his job. Almost everything came in and out of town through him.

Lou said goodbye, then ran to catch up with his parents.

He'd only been away five weeks, but when he walked into the house he felt like he hadn't seen it for years. Imagine how Georges was going to feel when he came home. Maman had baked six loaves of molasses bread and their scent filled the air. Fresh pine branches decorated all the window tops, adding to the smell. He could hear wood crackle in the kitchen stove. He couldn't wait to eat whatever Maman was cooking. Céline was a good cook, but no one cooked like Maman.

He ran up to his room and threw himself on his old bed. How good it would feel to sleep without fear of saying or doing something that would give him away, or of Claire coming too close. He stuffed his skirt way under the bed. He didn't want to see it for two weeks, until it was time to head back. He grabbed the gifts and money and headed to the kitchen.

"Oh, Alphonse, look. Have you ever seen anything as pretty?" Maman asked Papa when she unwrapped the sparkling star. She hung it on the window, under the branches, where it caught the sunlight.

When Papa opened his present, he just held it in his hand. Then Lou remembered that Papa couldn't read. "It's cream, for your cuts," said Lou.

"Isn't our son thoughtful? Here, let's try some on you," said Maman. She twisted the lid, scooped out a wad of cream, and sat beside Papa. She rubbed the lemony lotion into each of his hands, working gently over the cuts. Papa said nothing as he watched her work. Lou couldn't tell if he was happy or not. She took her time with each hand, like she was rubbing a whole lot of love into his skin along with the cream.

"Isn't that nice, Papa?" she asked.

Papa nodded and closed his eyes, looking more peaceful than he had since Georges left. Lou wondered what the last five weeks had been like for his parents, with no one but them in the house, except Mouffle. Lou had seen his father's face grow more and more worried over the year. Lou leaving too couldn't have helped. Now both his sons were far away from where he could protect them. Belgium or Montreal, what did it matter? In both places, his sons were out of reach.

Lou ran to Papa and did something he'd never done before. He hugged him and said, "It's so good to be home, Papa. Guess what? I met Newsy Lalonde. He actually shook my hand. This one." Lou held up his right hand.

"Really?" Papa grasped Lou's hand and held it in his own. Lou could see the nicks under the shiny cream and hoped his gift was doing some good already. Papa didn't let go the whole time Lou described his adventure at the Montreal Arena in delicious detail, the breakaways, the hits, the goals, even the fur rugs. And for once, Papa did not look down at the floor when Lou spoke.

Twenty-Seven

For the next few days, Lou ate like he'd been half-starved — quiche, tourtière, and, on his third night home, *bouili*. It was so good Lou ate three whole plate-fuls of the ham and vegetable roast. He leaned over his plate and shoveled the food in, barely chewing, not caring how much noise he made. Maman and Papa laughed as they watched the gravy dribble down his chin.

"What's the matter? Don't they have food in Montreal?" Papa asked.

"Tell us again how many goals you scored," said Maman.

"And this Lapensée. How could she be that good? She's just a girl, Louis."

"You still don't get it, Papa. These girls play. I mean, they really play. You should see Claire with the puck."

"Claire? Who's Claire? Don't let Francine know you have a crush," said Maman.

"I don't have a crush. I'm just telling you about

Claire. She's our best winger." Lou kept his face low, over the plate, in case he was blushing.

He wished his parents could see the team play. Then they'd understand. But Papa would never be able to picture the girls playing. He'd be seeing them the way Lou used to, slow and gentle, tripping over their feet. Maybe his parents could use some of the fifteen dollars to come to Montreal.

Maman refilled their glasses with hot cider. All they needed now was music, but there wouldn't be music in the house until Georges came home. He was the only one who could play the fiddle. Papa could sort of manage the spoons, and Maman could sing — not as well as she cooked, but she could carry a tune. Lou couldn't do anything but clap and tap his feet, but he loved it anyway.

Suddenly there was a knock at the front door, and it opened. Monsieur Geoffrion peeked around the wood. He pulled off his hat and bowed his head.

"*Pardon.* I am so sorry to come by so late. But we just got a telegram at the station. I'm sorry, Alphonse. It's for you."

Maman grabbed Lou's hand, and they both squeezed tight as Papa took the card from Monsieur Geoffrion. "Did you read it?" he asked his old friend. Monsieur Geoffrion nodded.

"I'm sorry. But yes, I did. It's hard not to, when they're coming in."

Papa handed the card across the table to Lou. Why didn't he just ask Monsieur Geoffrion what it said? Lou didn't want to read it, but he had no choice. The words were in English, so Lou read them to himself first to see if he could understand them. It was amazing how much English he had picked up just from being around the English players on the team and from listening to Madame Oliver. But now, at this moment, he wished with all his heart that he didn't understand a word of English, or of any language that could convey such a horrible message.

He took a deep breath and translated for his parents:

Deeply regret inform you Private Georges Lapierre injured. Being sent from England. Arrival December.

No one said a word. It was all so vague. Injured how? It must have been at Passchendaele, the place Lou had read about. How should they know what to expect? And when would he be back in December? It was already the twenty-third. There was only one week left to the month.

"I am so sorry, Alphonse, Angélique. *Mon dieu, mon dieu.*" Monsieur Geoffrion hung his head and bit his lips, like he didn't want any more blasphemy to escape. "I'll leave you now. But please, let me know if there is anything I can do."

They sat at the table, their hot cider growing cold. Lou thought about how much he'd wanted to tell Georges about his adventures. But how could he tell him about shaking Newsy Lalonde's hand now? And would Georges hear him if he did? Could he still hear?

"I have to go tell Audrée," Maman said, after what seemed like hours but was only minutes. "That poor girl. She has a right to know." Nobody argued. Lou and Papa listened to Maman pull on her coat and wrap a woolen scarf around her head. They heard her take a deep breath before opening the door to the cold. Maybe Lou should offer to go with her, to help guide her down the winding road past the church to Audrée's. But Maman might want to be alone. He wasn't sure.

Lou was sure of only one thing — the days were going to be agony until Georges came home.

Twenty-Eight

O n Christmas Eve, Lou and his parents made the long, winding walk beside the lake and down the hill to the white wooden church that stood in the center of town. Everyone would be there to hear midnight Mass. Father Béliveau would say all the usual things about the birth of Jesus and the sacrifice he had made so that all could live in peace and find salvation. And would they go visiting afterwards, from house to house, eating more and more tourtière and drinking more and more spiced wine or cocoa, all through the night? He had been looking forward to that, but not now.

News of Georges's injury had swept through the town. The women hugged Maman, wiping tears from their eyes with their mittens, and the men patted Papa on the back. No one had to use words. It was clear they were all thinking the same thing. If Georges could be injured, so could their sons. All the men in town had been told to report to a recruiting officer by mid-January. Conscription was going to happen.

"Lou." Someone was tapping him on the back. He turned to find Francine, looking prettier than ever in her green Christmas dress, her long dark hair falling down her back to the belt around her waist. Lou's present for her was in his pocket. He wanted to give it to her at the right moment.

Next thing he knew she was throwing her arms around him, and he was hugging her back.

"I'm so sorry about Georges, Lou," Francine said, so close he could feel her breath in his ear. "He'll be okay, you'll see. Maybe it's just a broken finger or something. You never know. Georges is so strong."

"Even a broken finger can ruin a hockey career, Francine."

Father Béliveau entered the pulpit, so Francine had to go find her family. "We'll talk later, okay, Lou?"

Audrée sat with Lou's family, holding Maman's hand. At the end of the sermon, Father Béliveau made everyone bow their heads and kneel one more time while he said a special prayer for Georges. "As you all know, St. George, who slew the devil when he slew the dragon, is the patron saint of soldiers. I am sure St. George was there with our own Georges when he battled the evils of Europe and that St. George protected him as best he could and that Georges will return to us with his faith in Jesus Christ our Lord wholly intact." The whole church murmured, "Amen."

How, Lou thought, *could Georges be whole when the telegram said he'd been injured?*

Everyone convinced Maman and Papa that they should not be alone, so they agreed to join the villagers as they shared food and cider with each other, singing carols as they walked from house to house. No one expected to be fed at Lou's house, though. Not this year.

He was glad when they reached Francine's. Her mother had made mulled wine with cloves and cinnamon. A big pot of it hung over the fireplace, filling the house with a spicy scent. Lou and Francine filled their mugs, then disappeared upstairs to the room Francine shared with her baby sister.

"So, how's the team?"

"It's great. I mean, the playing is great. And being in Montreal is great. We even went to see the Canadiens. But being a girl is hard."

"Tell me about it," said Francine. "Try being a girl with three younger siblings. And the girls? Do you like being with all those girls?"

Lou thought about Claire, with her beautiful blond hair and blue-green eyes, and the way she was always holding his hand and touching him, like that night in Ottawa. He hoped he wasn't blushing.

"No, not really," he replied. "I mean, they're nice and everything, but I'd rather not have to spend so much time with them."

"So much time? Don't you just play hockey with them?"

"Well, yeah, but I live with them too. I have to, no choice."

"And what do you mean by live? Like, in the same house?"

"Yes, and the same room." Francine pulled back and turned away. Maybe he shouldn't have told her that.

"And where do you sleep in this room?" she asked.

"Oh, Francine. In my own bed, far away from anyone else."

"For real?"

"Yes, for real. They all think I'm pretty weird, anyway, so they leave me alone." Lou was relieved that only part of this was a lie. "Anyway, enough about them. I want to forget it while I'm home. I have something for you." He pulled out the crinkly paper with Francine's present inside.

"For me?" Francine unwrapped the green ribbon and let it fall between her fingers. "Oh, Lou, it's so pretty. I've never had a ribbon for my hair. Would you help me?" She gathered up her dark hair in a ponytail and held it high up the back of her head, exposing her thin neck. "Tie it in the back for me, okay?"

Lou took the ribbon and tied it around her ponytail. There was no way to do it without touching her hair. His fingers were shaking. He'd done a hundred girlish things in the last two months. This shouldn't have been strange at all. But it was. And so was the way he was feeling.

Twenty-Nine

Monsieur Geoffrion said that Georges would most likely come in on the afternoon train. First he'd land in Halifax by boat. Then he'd be put on the overnight train that reached Montreal mid-morning. He'd connect with the train that left Montreal in the afternoon, switch in Ottawa, and be home soon after. If that's what happened. It was all only guesswork. They had not received another telegram with more specific details.

"The English soldiers' families probably get way more information," Papa said. "And even a real visit from someone important. But not us. Our soldiers get a piece of paper that tells us nothing, in English, like we don't matter. And they wonder why we're against conscription."

No one dared argue with him. With each passing day, Papa's mood turned heavier and heavier. Lou could see the tension gathering in his face, turning his cheeks hard as rock. Maman coped with the waiting by baking and cooking. It was like she was storing up enough food to feed Georges, and the rest of the 22nd Regiment, for a year.

Every day Maman and Lou walked to the train station to meet the afternoon train. Some days, when Papa could leave work early, he joined them. Audrée met them at the station if she could get out of her chores. She stood as quietly as they did, watching the track hopefully, her fingers kneading her handkerchief into a ball in her coat pocket.

Let it be today, thought Lou, standing on the platform one gray Saturday afternoon. *Coming here every day is getting too hard*. The telegram had said December, and there were only two days left in the month.

When the train turned into sight, Maman grabbed Lou's hand. Audrée had not joined them today. If she had, she and Maman would be gripping hands over their mittens. Papa was with them because it was the weekend. He was pacing from one end of the platform to the other. Monsieur Geoffrion squeezed Maman's shoulder on his way across to meet the train as it slowed to a stop, its brakes screeching.

The doors opened, but no one got off. Normally the conductor jumped out. Monsieur Geoffrion turned and shrugged, like he didn't get it either. Finally the conductor appeared and whispered something in Monsieur Geoffrion's ear. The station master looked over at Maman and nodded.

Oh my God! Georges is here!

Maman waved at Papa to come back. Where was he going? He was practically off the end of the platform. Lou couldn't stand it. Why wasn't Georges jumping off the train behind the conductor? Wasn't he happy to be home, even if he was hurt?

Suddenly a soldier appeared in the doorway. He was thinner than Georges and stooped. Georges was never stooped. Georges would have filled the entire doorway, side to side and top to bottom, like any good defenseman. The left leg of the soldier's pants was rolled up to his knee and clipped, which meant he had only half a leg. Lou watched as he placed his crutches very carefully on the stairs and swung down between them. When he was on the platform, another soldier behind him tossed a duffle bag down to Monsieur Geoffrion and saluted. Lou heard the soldier inside the train call out, *"Bonne chance*, Georges!"

When Maman heard the name, she dropped Lou's hand and darted over to her eldest son. Lou still couldn't move. He just stared at the half-leg, like the lower half would reappear if he looked hard enough. How would Georges skate without a leg? Georges was good at everything. There was nothing he couldn't do. But even he could not play hockey with only one leg.

Thirty

The scene at the train station was already a blur to Lou as he and his family walked home in the heavy falling snow, slower than ever because of Georges. There had been tears and hugs and handshakes and a few words, but Lou couldn't remember any of them. His brother's duffle bag was slung over his shoulder. It weighed a ton, but it was nothing compared to the weight that sat on his chest.

The first thing Georges did when he stepped into the house was to call for Mouffle, who came running. She rubbed against Georges's leg like she didn't even notice the other one was missing. Then she jumped into his arms, knocking over a crutch. Georges held her as she purred and licked his chin and nudged her nose against his cheeks.

It was like only the cat knew how to act.

Papa slumped in his special chair beside the kitchen stove and didn't say a word. Maman busied herself with pots and plates and cutlery. That left Lou alone at the table with Georges. What should he say? Even being a girl was easier than this. At Madame Oliver's he mostly copied what everyone else did. But he had no one to copy here. Georges was the first young man in town to come home injured in the war. That made Lou the first brother of an injured soldier.

Minutes later, Maman was laying out bowls of chicken soup. She cut a loaf of bread and a hunk of cheese onto a platter. Then she brought out a big bowl of potato salad. Papa finally joined them, and Maman sat down. But no one moved to eat a thing.

It was like an odd paralysis had settled over the table.

Maman looked like she was going to cry. She had obviously imagined Georges jumping at her home-made food, after months of eating army gruel. They had all spent the week trying to imagine what Georges's injuries were, but never once did Lou picture a missing leg. Broken, yes. But missing, no.

Why wouldn't Georges speak? Why didn't Papa ask him to?

Finally, Georges cleared his throat. It was scratchy, like he hadn't spoken in a long time. "It's all right, everyone. At least I'm home. Not everyone else was so lucky." He didn't sound like Georges, who was normally so loud, everything sounding like a declaration tinged with humor. This was more of a whimper.

"Oh, Georges," said Maman, wiping her eyes. "You *are* home. Look, Papa. Our son is home. Georges is home."

But Papa still didn't look up. Lou had thought his face would soften once Georges was home, but it hadn't. It was harder than ever, with cracks along his forehead. Finally Papa threw down his spoon. "He is home, but he didn't have to leave in the first place. Look at him. And now what? No leg. No job. No future."

"Papa!" cried Lou. This couldn't be what Georges wanted to hear. Still, he thought of Boss at the port in Montreal. All his workers had two legs. Papa might be right. What kind of work could Georges do with only one?

"All for the English war," Papa continued.

Georges stood up, pushing against the table with his good leg, making his soup slosh over the rim of the bowl. "It wasn't only the English war, Papa. You're wrong. It was French and Belgian and Dutch and Italian and Russian all fighting the Germans and their allies. The world is a big place, much bigger than this little town."

"Only if you let it be," said Papa.

"Well, I chose to let it be, Papa. Women and children were being killed, thousands of them. We had to help. We had to stop the Germans. What kind of men are we if we just let those things happen?"

"What kind of man are you now, with only one leg?"

Lou sucked in his breath, hard, like Papa's words

had knocked all the oxygen out of the room. He watched in horror as Maman reached across the table and slapped Papa across the face.

Never in his entire life had he seen such a thing.

Thirty-One

Lou waited and waited for Georges to come upstairs. His brother's bed stood across from his own,
completely empty. Maman had gone to bed shortly
after the uneaten dinner, and Papa had left the house,
most probably to take refuge at Monsieur Geoffrion's. If
what Maman had done to Papa made its way around
town, Father Béliveau wouldn't be happy. Wives hitting
their husbands. Women making bombs in factories.
Girls playing hockey. What was next? Women actually
voting? Lou could hear the whole sermon in his head.

Finally Lou went downstairs. Maybe Georges didn't
plan to share a room with him anymore. Maybe he
didn't want to undress in front of anyone and reveal
his half-leg. Lou knew what it was like to want to hide,
but he needed to know what had happened to his
brother.

Georges was lying on the sofa under one of Maman's
knit blankets, with Mouffle sprawled across his stomach.

It was dark, with only the light of a dying fire in the wood stove across the hall to light the room, so Lou couldn't see where the injured leg stopped short under the wool.

"Hey, Georges. Are you okay?" asked Lou, sitting across from him on the rocker.

"We'll see, little brother," Georges replied softly, not shifting an inch. Maybe he had gotten used to lying perfectly still in the trenches.

"Was it awful?"

"It was worse than awful."

"Worse than you thought?"

"I didn't think. That's the trouble."

"What do you mean?"

"War's not a game. That's what I thought it would be, a game. Two sides, one against the other. Everyone with the same equipment, with rules to follow, maybe even a referee to decide. But that's not how it was. There's no such thing as fair in war. It's just chaos."

"So what happened to you?"

"We were at the front, trying to hold back the Germans, and I took some bad fire in my leg. A round of mortar. They couldn't save it."

"Did it hurt?"

"I don't remember. I passed out."

"Well, I'm glad you're back, Georges. Papa is glad too. He's just scared. He doesn't want either of us to go, ever."

"You? Where would you go, Petit Lou?"

"You don't know, I guess?"

"Know what?"

Lou wanted to tell him, but he didn't want to at the same time. Hockey meant as much to Georges as it did to Lou, maybe more. Georges was supposed to make it to the NHA first, then help Lou follow later. That had always been the plan.

"I joined a hockey team in Montreal. A real one, with a coach and uniforms."

"No way! A team for players your age?"

"Yes, but ..." Lou felt a complete fool saying it. What would Georges think? Georges's story was about bravery and heroism. He was trying to help save innocent people from being killed. Lou's story was about lying and cheating. He wasn't saving anyone. In fact, he was hurting whichever girl would have taken his spot on the team. And Georges's opinion mattered to him more than anyone else's. But he'd find out sooner or later.

"It's a girls' team," he said.

Even in the dark, Lou could make out the silhouette of Georges's jaw dropping open.

Thirty-Two

When Lou came back downstairs the next morning, Audrée was there, sitting on the end of the sofa with Georges's head in her lap. She must have come over early, while everyone was still asleep. She was running her fingers through Georges's hair. When she stroked his face and down his neck Lou didn't know where to look. It surprised him even more to find Maman and Papa awake and sitting in the kitchen, acting as if Georges and his girlfriend were not together on the sofa ten feet away. Papa must have come back sometime in the night, after Lou and Georges had stopped talking.

"Bless that girl," Maman was saying as she buttered bread, hot from the oven. "It doesn't matter to her." Maman's eyes were red and puffy.

"Hmph," grunted Papa. "It doesn't now. But wait until she needs to feed her children."

"Georges said there will be a pension from the army.

They'll manage. If they love each other, it's all that matters."

"Love. Hmph ... Love doesn't buy food. And if that eldest son of ours still believes a word the English say ..." Papa was standing now, waving his arms. His face was set like stone, with lines chiseled around his eyes and down his cheeks.

Maman was about to shout back when Audrée stepped into the kitchen. Her face looked fresh and even cheerful.

"Maman and Papa, Georges may have lost a leg, but he didn't lose his hearing. This is *not* helping. Your son is alive. Isn't that enough? Now, give me a plate of bread, please. Georges and I want to eat our breakfast in peace." They all watched as Audrée, her dark hair hanging loose down her back, piled a few slices of Maman's bread on a plate.

"She is as delusional as he is," said Papa finally. "I'm going out."

Lou sat across from Maman, who was now frying up eggs with ham and onions. It surprised him when Audrée shouted out from the living room, "Smells good, Maman. Real good." Georges and Audrée had been sweethearts since they were fourteen, not much older than Lou. Everyone knew they'd get married one day. That was just the way it worked. When he'd first seen Georges get off the train, Lou had thought that might have changed, but judging from the sound of

Audrée's voice, he guessed not. She sounded like she always did. Lou looked across the kitchen and past the doorway into the living room. He couldn't believe what he saw. Audrée was rubbing the cream Lou had bought his father into Georges's stump. Lou couldn't help staring. The end of Georges's leg was crude and bumpy, like dough folded over during the kneading. But Audrée didn't flinch. She was taking her time, as though it was the most beautiful piece of skin she'd ever touched.

Maman set a plate of eggs in front of Lou, then started off toward the living room with another. Audrée called out, "No, Maman. Give us a minute. We're coming to the table. This son of yours has to learn that he won't be served hand and foot." Two minutes later, Georges and Audrée appeared. Georges was walking with one crutch, his left pant leg rolled and pinned. Audrée held up his other side. His face was down, like he didn't want to see where he was going.

When everyone had a plate of food, Maman insisted on saying grace. "*Merci Dieu* for the food we are about to eat. *Merci Dieu* for bringing my son home from the war. *Merci Dieu* that me and Papa are healthy, and please guide Papa in a better direction. *Merci Dieu* for Audrée, who is surely an angel in disguise, and *merci Dieu* that Lou Lou, my baby, is home too."

Audrée set a plate of food in front of Georges and handed him a fork. Normally Georges dove into Maman's food, shoveling it in as fast as she could dish it out. But today he ate slowly, taking small bites and chewing the food cautiously, like he wasn't sure what it was. Could six months of bad army food have made him forget Maman's cooking? The lines of Georges's ribs showed through his undershirt. He was skinnier than Lou had ever seen him.

Why wasn't Maman saying anything? Lou was sure that if she spoke first, Georges would answer and they could start talking like they used to, the words flying around the table faster than the butter, salt, and apple juice. But when Lou looked at Maman he could see that she wasn't looking up either, and she was taking even smaller bites than Georges. It was like everyone was afraid their eggs would explode if their teeth came down too hard. He suddenly regretted that he'd taken such a big mouthful himself.

"This is so good, Maman; isn't it, Georges?" said Audrée finally. "Especially with that touch of maple syrup that you add to the eggs. Only you know how to make ham and eggs taste so sweet."

"It's true, Maman. No one cooks like you," Lou added. Lou wanted to say something about Céline's cooking at Madame Oliver's, how it had been good but not nearly as good as Maman's, but that would mean talking about the team in front of Audrée. The only people who knew, outside of the family, were Francine and probably Monsieur Geoffrion. It was best to keep it that way.

The compliments only managed to put a tiny smile on Maman's face. It was like she was waiting for a word of approval from one person only, Georges. Until he enjoyed it, she couldn't either, no matter who else found her food delicious.

The sounds of Papa chopping wood out in the shed pounded through the kitchen walls, as if the house had a heartbeat. It was slight, but every time the ax struck wood Georges's shoulders lurched forward and his eyelids pinched. Did the sound remind him of something that had happened in Belgium? Or maybe it was the thought that Georges might never be able to chop wood for Audrée and their children — that simple task that all the men in Saint-Christophe performed throughout the year. Chopping wood. It would be next to impossible to retain his balance on one leg and chop wood, and even more impossible if one arm had to support a crutch.

"My goodness, Lou, your hair sure is long," said Audrée in a loud voice, like she was trying hard to drown out the chopping.

At the mention of Lou's name, Georges looked over at his little brother. Their eyes had not locked yet, not since Lou's confession last night. Lou felt a piece of ham lodging in his throat. What did Georges think of him? He had to know.

"Maman, why do you let him go around with such long hair? People will think he's a girl," Audrée continued. "It's long enough to braid. You could turn it into a rug."

Suddenly Georges laughed. It wasn't his old laugh, bouncing off the ceiling, but it was enough of a laugh to fill the table. Maman's eyes flashed between her sons, full of hope.

"Well, as long as you don't start wearing dresses, little brother," Georges said, winking at Lou.

"Georges, leave Lou alone. You're making him blush," Audrée urged, poking him in the ribs. "Besides, I'm sure he has to put it up in one of those funny white hats at the bakery. Am I right, Lou?"

Lou swallowed. It was clear that she didn't know. Georges hadn't told her. They had obviously shared a lot of things on the sofa that morning, but Lou's secret wasn't one of them.

Thirty-Three

The following days settled into a rhythm, as steady as Papa's wood chopping. Georges continued to sleep on the sofa in the living room, but nobody minded. It was better than watching him struggle up the steep, narrow stairs on one leg. They rarely used that room anyway, preferring to huddle in the warmth of the kitchen. Georges slept until eight, rising only after Papa had already left for the sawmill. Audrée showed up soon after and helped Georges wash and dress. Then she spent the mornings, sometimes helping Maman in the kitchen, but mostly talking with Georges. A couple of times Lou caught her stroking Georges's hair or rubbing his neck again. If she was still massaging cream into his stump, he hadn't noticed.

Audrée was there the day a letter came from the army, addressed to Georges. Normally Monsieur Geoffrion brought the mail to the supply store in town, which doubled as a post office. But since this was for Georges, he'd walked it over in between trains.

"Do you want to open it?" Audrée asked Georges, holding it in front of his face.

"No. You do it," said Georges, staring down at his hands. Maybe he was afraid he was being called back into service, but that would be impossible with one leg.

Lou and Maman gathered around as Audrée read the English letter, stopping to translate, as much as she could, with Lou's help. The letter was informing Georges that he was eligible to go to Montreal for a fitting for an artificial leg. It was supposed to be "the latest in prosthetic technology, one hundred percent guaranteed" to help Georges "walk like a full-limbed person."

Maman and Audrée hugged each other. "Oh, Georges. Wait until Papa hears," said Maman. "He'll be so pleased, and so surprised. The English are taking care of you after all."

"Yes, Georges. It's wonderful. And they say it won't cost you a penny," added Audrée. "And it'll make such a difference, you'll see. You'll be like nor—." Audrée stopped herself, but not until it was too late.

Georges's face turned dark, and he almost spat out the words as he spoke. "Normal. That's what you were going to say. *Normal*. So you think I'm not normal. You're just bouncing around me, pretending that I am. Don't forget the leg will be wood. There won't be any blood flowing through it. It will still be cold to touch. Is that normal?" Georges turned himself around on the sofa, folded his arms over his chest, and closed his eyes. "I want you all to leave me alone now, okay?"

"But, Georges," said Audrée, close to tears. Maman pulled her gently by the arm into the kitchen.

"Let him be for a while, *chérie*. He didn't mean it." Audrée grabbed her coat and left, her boots crunching down the road on the icy snow. Lou and Maman felt Georges's presence in the living room, heavy as steel without Audreé there to lighten him up.

With Georges's back turned, Lou took advantage and dragged his new skates out from under his bed. He hadn't laced them up once since Georges's return. The very presence of skates would be cruel in front of his brother, who would probably never skate again, even with a wooden leg.

Lou knocked twice on Francine's door then opened it, as was the custom. No need to wait to be let in, like at Madame Oliver's. Francine's home was his home and vice versa, like all the houses in the village. He found her in the hall, washing her brother's and sisters' faces.

"Can you come?" asked Lou, holding up his skates. They hadn't skated together since the night before he'd left for Montreal, when they'd kissed under the big pines. He wondered if Francine was thinking that too.

"I can't, Lou, not unless I bring these guys along." She pointed at her siblings, who were now wrapped around her legs like three giant cats. Lou could see

Francine's mother in the kitchen, stirring a pot of laundry on the stove.

"Better than nothing," Lou said. "I'll help." They grabbed coats, scarves, mitts, and hats and suited up the kids, who were bouncing with excitement. Only Francine had skates. The little ones had pieces of cardboard to glide on.

It was a beautiful early January day, cold, crisp, and sunny. The ice shone like glass, and when their skates sprayed up slivers, they sparkled like crystal. Lou wished he could take Francine's hand and skate her over to the other side, to the tall pines, but he couldn't. They had to watch the kids. He had so much he wanted to tell her. Seeing Georges turned in on himself on the sofa, like a slug in a shell, when he should be out here with Lou, practicing his shot-blocking techniques, made him want to cry. Could he really break down and cry in front of Francine? Papa said men didn't cry, and that must be true. Lou had never seen Papa cry. And even though Georges sometimes looked like he wanted to, he hadn't.

"Give me your hand, Lou," Francine said. "We'll skate together, in small circles. The kids are all right." They had found a pile of snow they could slide down, onto the lake.

Holding Francine's hand was just what Lou needed. How did she always know, like Audrée? It must be a sixth sense girls had.

They skated round and round in the sunshine, matching each other stride for stride. Lou knew this was how Georges and Audrée had started out. It was how most couples started out in Saint-Christophe, on the ice. If things continued this way, they would end up married one day, not even that far away. Maman and Papa had married at seventeen. The thought didn't scare him that much. He could still play hockey, even married to Francine. She'd live in the big city with him, and he'd buy her modern things, like a fancy stove and one of those new ring-washers for washing clothes like Céline used at Madame Oliver's, so she wouldn't have to work as hard as her mother did. Francine would cheer him on from the stands, sitting in a special place, on a thick fur rug, calling out his name.

But Audrée would never do the same for Georges. And Georges wouldn't be a teammate, not the way they had always planned.

Lou felt a few tears squeeze out of his eyes and freeze on his face. What would Francine say if she saw them?

Suddenly she was taking off her mitts and placing her warm hands on his face, one cheek at a time. "Oh, Lou. Georges will be fine. He just needs time."

"But he was so brave, going away like that to fight to save people's lives. He was a real hero. And now …" He couldn't finish.

"There are many ways of being a hero, Lou," Francine said, pulling her mittens back on.

Lou thought about that as they continued to skate, making it almost all the way across to the pines before Francine's siblings called them back, complaining that they were cold.

Thirty-Four

A few days into January, a letter arrived for Lou. Monsieur Geoffrion did not walk this one over to the house. Papa picked it up on his way home from work. It was from the Oliver Bakery. The logo, three fat-cheeked chefs in tall white hats, sat in the corner.

Lou opened the letter. No one hovered over him to hear what it said.

The Bakers will be starting the second half of the season on January 10. The team will play ten more games up to the end of March, two against the Vics, two against the Flyers, two against the Alerts, and end with four straight against our Montreal rivals, the Westerns. You will find enclosed a train ticket to Montreal and a five-dollar bonus. Please call Madame Oliver and let her know when you plan to arrive so she can meet you at Windsor Station. We look forward to a successful second half of the season and to seeing you soon.

Monsieur Oliver.

Lou stared at the letter for a long time. Somehow, Monsieur Oliver and his bakery and the entire team seemed so far away. Had he really dressed as a girl for five whole weeks? It seemed impossible. And this would be for longer, at least ten weeks. Lou's favorite days had been Sundays, his days of freedom. But could those continue? Not that he hadn't loved every minute out on the ice, playing hockey. Somehow, when he was playing he forgot that Claire, Bernadette, Danielle, and all the others were girls. They were simply his teammates.

Lou pocketed the money quickly, before anyone could see. This was his money, no one else's, especially if no one was going to show any interest.

He did tell Francine about the letter later that day. They skated every afternoon while the kids slid on their hill, squealing as they zoomed onto the lake on their bellies. If Georges felt bad about Lou going out to skate, he didn't let on.

"I'm sorry you're leaving again," said Francine.

"You are, but nobody else cares," answered Lou. "I had so much I wanted to tell Georges about it all, but he doesn't seem interested."

"Poor Lou," said Francine. Every day they made it closer and closer to the pine trees where they'd first kissed.

"I wish you were coming," he said. "That would make me want to go back for sure."

"Well, you know I can't. And besides, it would blow your cover. Imagine skating like this? Or this?" Francine dropped Lou's hand and spun around, digging the toe of her skate into the ice, her right leg landing gracefully behind her. She reached up and kissed Lou on the lips. The kiss was like a blast of heat. Lou put his arms around her and pulled her close, blocking out the wind. He could stay like this all day and never go back inside, into the cold house.

"I'll miss you, Lou."

"And I'll miss you."

They skated back to the kids, whose cries were growing louder. They could never stay out for more than an hour without starting to freeze. Lou's toes were also burning, but he didn't care. He'd let them frostbite and fall off if it meant more time with Francine. He stood back and watched her lift her siblings, one at a time, rubbing their backs to get their blood going. She blew hot breath on their fingers, their mittens in her hand, crusted with ice. She reminded him of his mother, always trying to make everyone comfortable. And of Audrée, whose patience stretched as far as the lake, even on days when Georges did little more than grunt at her.

Was it something girls were born with, this talent for looking after other people? He thought of Claire and the other girls. He remembered them talking about their year of hockey like it would be their only great adventure before they turned themselves over to caring for others, either as nuns or mothers.

And then here he was, thinking night and day about only one thing — how he could still become a hockey star now that Georges had lost a leg.

For the first time, it occurred to Lou that maybe he could do more than just dress up like a girl. Maybe he could act like one too and try taking care of someone other than himself. Instead of waiting for Georges to come around and turn into his old self, as least as much as he was able, maybe Lou could help make that happen.

"I'll see you tomorrow, Francine," Lou said at her door. He made sure no one was looking and kissed her on the cheek, which was red as a radish. Then, instead of going home, he turned toward the center of town.

"Well, well, hello, Louis," said Monsieur Geoffrion, sitting in his tiny office, a tin heater full of coal at his feet. The air smoked around his face as he spoke. "What brings you here? And when do you head back to work? They sure do give you a generous amount of time off at that bakery." Monsieur Geoffrion winked.

"They let me stay longer when I told them about Georges," Lou said, amazed that he could lie so easily, especially to Papa's oldest friend. Maybe there was no need to lie, but Lou didn't feel like talking about the Bakers right now. He was here for Georges, not himself. "I need to buy a ticket please. Montreal return."

"Yes, sir. Here you go. Two-fifty, please." Lou felt good handing over his five-dollar bill.

The letter had said Georges could stay at the hospital during his fitting, so he wouldn't need money for a room or food. Now all he needed to do was convince Georges to go.

Thirty-Five

Audrée was able to stay for dinner, and Lou was glad. Georges was slightly less closed up when she was around.

"Doesn't your maman make the best quiche, Georges? Even my maman, who's a good cook, doesn't make it this tasty. I'm going to steal all your recipes for when I cook for Georges," she said to Maman, smiling at Georges.

"And when will that be?" said Papa. Everyone stiffened. It was hard to tell if he meant it in a good way, like when are you guys actually getting married, or in a mean way. Like, that will only happen when hell freezes over.

"As soon as possible, right, Georges?" Audrée placed her hand over Georges's and squeezed it. Georges said nothing.

"You'll make a beautiful bride, Audrée," Maman said. "And Georges, of course, will be a handsome groom."

Lou sucked in his breath. It was the type of comment Georges could lash back at, playing up the image of him stumping down the aisle. Or Papa could say something too, especially today. Monsieur Geoffrion had told him this morning that a government official was coming to town at the end of next week to sign up young men. Conscription was here. No one dared mention the word. It would be like an explosion in the middle of the table, as strong as the one that had injured Georges.

"And you'll make beautiful babies," said Maman, making Audrée blush. Lou knew Georges and Audrée used to hang out in the field across the lake, even though Father Béliveau had warned them not to. But now, even though Audrée was always touching Georges, he never touched her, at least not in front of anyone. Maybe that was something else that Georges needed time for. It was like his new body was a uniform, one he had to get accustomed to wearing.

"Maybe a spring wedding, right, Georges?" said Audrée. "It's what we always planned."

"Yes, but that was before," said Georges. "Why do you keep pretending nothing's changed?" He banged his fork onto his plate.

"But nothing has," said Audrée.

Georges jumped up and pushed back his chair so quickly, it made Lou choke. He had no idea his brother could still move like that. "Look at this," he said. "Doesn't this look different?" He was pointing to his left leg, where the material was rolled and clipped. "It changes everything, no matter how much you want to pretend it doesn't. There's so much I can't do now. I can't ..." Georges' words trailed off, like he couldn't decide which of the many things he couldn't do to start with. His lips were quivering, like the list was a logjam vibrating against them.

"But, Georges, I still want —"

"I know you do, Audrée," said Georges. "But I don't want this for you. Papa is right. I'm not a man anymore. I can't do any of the things a man should do for you."

Lou heard the sound before he noticed where it was coming from. It was soft like a baby's gurgle. At first he thought it might be Mouffle under the table, lapping at Georges's foot. But then he saw. It was Papa, his hands clasped like fists in front of his face, crying softly.

Why now, when Georges had said he was right? Didn't he want to be right? Wasn't he glad that he had been right about Georges ruining his life when he enlisted all those months ago?

Nobody dared say a word. But Lou was sure they were all feeling it, as though Papa's sobs were part of them, shaking them deep down inside at the very center of their beings.

Thirty-Six

In the middle of the night, Lou heard noises out on the lake. Could it be wolves, or even stray dogs, their claws scratching on the ice? He threw on his clothes, grabbed his coat, hat, and mitts, and headed outside. He needed to breathe open air. The smoky air in the house was choking him. The moon and bright white snow guided him to the lake in the dark. The lake always shone, even if the moon was just a sliver. Somehow it was enough to catch and light up the ice. He sat on the hill and looked out. He could make out a figure, too tall to be a wolf. Maybe it was a bear, in which case he should turn around and quietly head back home. But bears hibernated, so that couldn't be it.

Lou stepped gingerly onto the ice to get a closer look.

He couldn't believe what he saw. It was Georges, skating on the lake in the middle of the night. He was gliding with his good leg, which was in a boot, then using a piece of cloth that looked like one of Maman's old kitchen rags tied to the tip of the crutch to glide with the other. He was surprisingly fast. Not like the old Georges, but pretty good.

"I see you, little brother," Georges called out suddenly. "You're not as quiet as you think."

"Sorry. But hey, that's pretty good."

"It's not bad, but I can't hold a stick."

"I know, but still. The skating is good."

"Stop trying to be nice, Lou. I like it better when you're pestering me, like old times."

Lou laughed. "Like when I'd fill your skates with flour? Or rub ashes all over your stick so the ice would turn black around you?"

"Yeah, like that."

They glided around each other for a while, listening to owls hooting in the trees.

"So, this team of yours. You really play with girls?"

"Yep. I know it's crazy, but I wanted to beat this girl, Albertine Lapensée. She's insanely good. Super fast and crafty."

"I think you've gone soft, little brother. A girl? How big is she?"

"Bigger than me," said Lou.

"A mouse is bigger than you." Lou used to hate it when his brother mocked his size, but tonight it felt good.

"So, show me how fast you can skate, now that you've been out there with a bunch of girls."

"Now?"

"Sure. Why not? It's perfect out here." Georges was right. The air was crisp and fresh, and the whole town was silent. It was as if he and Georges were the only people alive and the bright strip of lake was the entire world.

"Okay, I'll be back." Lou ran home and grabbed his skates off the porch. Back at the lake he laced them up quickly. He didn't need to see. He could do it all by feel. Georges was still skating around. This time Lou could see that he was wobbly. The crutch was hard to steady. One slip and Georges would be down. It would be hard for him to get up on his own.

"Ready, little brother?" called Georges from across the lake. He was only shadow now, like a tree.

Lou started across. He'd never grow tired of that sound. The blade cutting into the ice, slicing it. The ice pushing back, propelling him forward, like a helping hand. Georges was growing clearer, standing perfectly still. Suddenly, Lou saw himself through his brother's eyes. Petit Lou, as he'd always been known, now skating faster than Georges ever would. He felt his legs grow heavy and he slowed down, skidding to a halt beside his brother.

"Not bad, little brother. But why'd you slow down? You were really moving at first."

"I don't know. Out of practise, I guess."

"Bull. You slowed down because of me, didn't you? Nobody knows how to act around me anymore."

"Sorry, Georges. It's just, you know, the whole hockey thing."

"Lou," Georges said, placing his hands on Lou's shoulders. "Don't you know? I want you to make it more than ever now, for both of us."

Lou didn't know what to say. All he knew was that they were supposed to make it together, the most famous brother duo the Canadiens would ever know, even if the team lasted a hundred years.

"It'll be hard without you, Georges. You taught me everything I know on the ice. Everything. I don't know if I can do it without you."

Now it was Georges's turn to be quiet. After a while he said, "But you went off to Montreal without me."

"I went because you went. You were having this big adventure, so I wanted one too. But if you're just lying at home ..." The owls were hooting like crazy atop the pine trees. Maybe they were sharing their dreams too. "I still need you, Georges. With one leg or two. It doesn't matter. But two would be better because you could do more. If only you'd get that wooden leg. It would help, you know it would. And I'll be there too. You can come with me when I go back. And you can come see our team. You should see the Victoria Rink where we play. It's incredible."

"See you fly around the ice in a skirt. I'd go for that."

"Good, then here. I have something for you." Lou pulled the train ticket out of his coat pocket. He'd been looking all night for the right moment to give it to Georges, and this was it. Somewhere in the distance wolves howled, as though they agreed.

"Tickets to Montreal, eh? You got these all by yourself?"

"Yeah."

"You are growing up, Petit Lou. Pray this war is over in less than five years, though. And that there are no more."

"If you promise to go to Montreal, I'll pray every night, Georges."

Georges held out his free hand, nearly losing his balance. "Deal," he said. "I need all the prayers I can get."

Thirty-Seven

Maman, Papa, and Audrée all waved goodbye as the train pulled away from Saint-Christophe. Lou's Bakers' uniform lay in his bag, ready to pull on, but he wouldn't do that right away, not like last time. He hadn't called Madame Oliver to tell her he was coming. He would just show up when he was good and ready. He didn't officially have to be there for another four days. He planned to use his time wisely.

"Welcome home, son," said the man who punched their tickets, bowing toward Georges, who was wearing his army uniform. The man spoke English, but still, he smiled at Georges as though he really were his son.

A pretty young mother with a little boy asked if her son could shake his hand. "*S'il vous plait,*" she pled, like it was really important to her. But when the boy asked if he could see Georges's leg, the woman yanked him away. "*Ce n'est pas poli,*" they heard her say.

"Don't worry," said Georges. *"Il n'est qu'un enfant."*

Georges was right. He *was* just a kid. War must seem fun to someone that age, like playing cowboys and Indians. He himself had thought that, not so long ago.

At some point, a group of soldiers walked through the car. When they saw Georges, they stopped and saluted. He stood up and did the same back.

"Coming or going?" asked Georges.

"Going," they said together.

Georges's jaw stiffened. *"Bonne chance,"* he said, saluting again.

It was clear that Georges's leg had turned him into a hero. And Georges acted more like one here, on the train, than he had at home. Maybe it was because of how people were treating him. It was the way people treated Lou after a great game, like the reporter had, or even his teammates or girls from other teams. Lou wondered if it made Georges feel as good inside.

At Windsor Station, Lou found them a taxi to take them up the steep hill to the Royal Victoria Hospital, where Georges would get his new leg. Lou had seen the hospital from afar, sitting like a gray stone castle with all its spires and turrets, tall and imposing, at the side of Mount Royal.

The staff was nice. Two nurses took Georges right in and settled him in a ward with other war-wounded.

"Where will you stay?" Georges asked when Lou was saying goodbye. "With that baker's sister?"

"Not yet, Georges. But don't worry about me. I know my way around. I'll come see you tomorrow."

Lou sped right down to the docks. He walked up to Boss's shed and knocked, but there was no answer. He was probably out with Jean, making deliveries. Lou used a bit of his money to buy a pastry and hot chocolate. He huddled against the shed door to eat, out of the cold wind, tucking his bag in behind him. The port was quieter than it had been just before Christmas. There were fewer ships tied up to the wharfs and much less box-tossing going on.

"Well, well, if it isn't the little man, Lou. You abandon us for weeks, then you show up again, eh? Looking for work, I suppose."

"Sorry, Boss. I had to go home. My brother was injured in the war."

"*Désolé*," said Boss. "That's rough. Okay, let's open her up, see what we have."

Lou gasped. He thought Boss meant his bag, but when he looked up he saw Boss opening the huge pad-lock that kept his shed secure.

"Over there. See those piles of leather strips? All scrap. But you know what they say about one man's garbage?" Lou nodded, even though he didn't. "It's another man's treasure. Got these by hard graft, going from shop to shop. I need someone to sort them by color and size. Then we're gonna bundle them and sell them off, see?"

Lou nodded. He could learn a lot from Boss. The man had ideas, maybe some he could share with Georges.

"I'm going home. You can stay as late as you want. There's a lamp there in the corner, and you can throw some lumps of coal in the stove. But you won't be able to come and go, because I have the key and I don't give that to anyone. You understand?"

"Yes, Boss." This would be perfect. He'd work through the night and stay here. It would be cold, even with the small stove, but he could always nestle under the larger scraps of leather. With any luck, he could spend the next few days like this. He'd sort and let his mind wander. He'd think about what he was doing. Part of him couldn't wait to get back on the rink, to be scoring goals. But a whole other part of him dreaded it. The first time it had just been fear, wondering if he could really pull off pretending to be a girl for so long. Now that he knew he could, something else was nagging at him. Something bigger. But he needed time to sort out what it was.

Thirty-Eight

For three days Lou sorted leather and slept. When Boss let him out in the mornings he grabbed some food, then ran up the hill to visit Georges. He watched the nurse secure the harness around Georges's waist. The harness was attached to a leather strap that circled Georges's thigh. From there, a rod ran down to the wooden leg that extended below Georges's knee, shaped exactly like a real one. Georges leaned against the nurse and began to walk. He wasn't the only one. At least a dozen men were also learning to use new arms or legs. Lou sat on Georges's bed and watched them all working with the nurses, taking tentative steps or pulling wooden arms through shirt sleeves. He wondered what each man's story was. Had they been wounded like Georges had, by shellfire, or had it been bombs or other weapons that Lou didn't even know?

"Hey, Georges. Is this Petit Lou?" called a man whose moustache covered his entire mouth and half his cheeks. Georges nodded from where he lay on his bed, taking a break, and Lou prayed his brother hadn't told everyone why he was in the city. Imagine all these war heroes knowing that he dressed up as a girl. He'd die.

"Here, play catch with me. Pretend it's a loaf of bread." The man used steel hooks on the end of his wooden arms to pick up a large leather ball. As he tossed it he shouted, "Catch, baker boy." Lou almost missed, he was so relieved Georges had kept his secret safe. He threw the ball back, wondering what it would be like not to have hands to grasp it.

"Hey, Sister. Think I could try out for the Yankees yet?" The man laughed as he released the ball into the air. It soared over Georges's bed straight for Lou. The nurse applauded.

"They'd be foolish to turn you down, Guillaume," she replied, smiling. The man had called her Sister, and that made Lou wonder if she was a nun. Maybe this is what Claire would do one day, work with wounded soldiers. He tried to picture her walking slowly around the large room, a soldier leaning against her as he l earned to put down his wooden leg. But he couldn't. It was impossible to imagine Claire doing anything other than speeding down the ice on his right side, looking for an opening to either pass or shoot, her blond curls whipping behind her.

Lou and Guillaume tossed the ball back and forth for a while, until Guillaume said, "That's it, kid. I can't do any more," and sank onto his bed. A poster hung above Guillaume's bed stand. On it was a picture of a gymnast hurtling himself over a vault. Across the bottom, it said, "George Eyser, Gold Medal, Vault, 1904 Olympics." It was incredible how high this Eyser guy could jump. But what was more incredible was that he had a wooden leg.

"Pretty amazing, eh, kid?" said Guillaume, tipping his head back to see the poster.

"Yeah," said Lou. "It sure is."

"I threw it up there for inspiration. For me and ... well ... for the whole team, really. Right, Georges?" Guillaume spoke to Georges, but winked at Lou, as if they were in on something. Lou looked at his brother, hoping to see him smile. Georges never walked on his wooden leg for long when Lou was there. Other guys seemed to be trying harder, but Lou would never say that out loud.

"Sure, Guillaume, I'll try out for the national team next month," said Georges. "Maybe for the high jump." Lou drew in his breath. If only Georges could sound more optimistic and stop poking fun at himself.

"Then I'll go with you," responded Guillaume. "You, me, and everyone. I could hold a javelin with these." Guillaume held up the steel hooks.

Lou braced himself for a nasty barb from his brother, but what came instead was laughter.

"You're too much, Guillaume. I can't be down with

you around," said Georges.

"Good, then get up. Show your brother what you can do."

Lou was amazed when Georges said, "Okay" and called for the nurse. She came over and helped him up. Then they walked the perimeter of the room slowly, with Guillaume and a few other soldiers clapping every time they turned a corner.

It would have been so much harder for Georges to do this at home, on his own. The men needed each other, like a real team. As he watched his brother try to retain his balance, Lou wondered what would happen if he didn't go back to the Bakers. Coach would shuffle Marie-Claude up to center for Claire and Bernadette, but Lapensée would make mincemeat of her. They'd come so close to beating the Vics — one more try and Lou was sure they could do it.

Thirty-Nine

The next day, on his way out of the hospital, Lou ducked into a washroom and pulled on his girls' clothes. He had said goodbye to Boss and brought his bag with him. It was time to go back to Madame Oliver's, for the sake of the team. He tied his hair back in a long ponytail, letting it fall free under his tuque. He couldn't do anything about the clunky boots he wore under the skirt, or the baggy torn coat, but the girls were used to those things on Lou. Luckily, in the big city, no one paid anyone else much attention.

When Lou got to the corner of Peel and Sherbrooke, every muscle in his body wanted to turn south, back to the docks. He had to force himself to continue west, toward Madame Oliver's. He closed his eyes and took a deep breath at the bottom of the stairs before climbing them to ring the bell.

"Lou Lou! Madame Oliver, it's Lou Lou. She's back," cried Danielle, running halfway down the hall to the kitchen, then turning back again, like she couldn't decide where to go.

Madame Oliver appeared, looking as elegant as ever in a high-collared green blouse with a string of pearls across the buttons. "Lou Lou? Oh my God. How did you get here? Why didn't you call? You didn't come alone, did you?"

"I did. I took a taxi. It was no big deal."

"Oh my, you young ladies are so independent these days. Even Danielle keeps insisting on walking downtown alone to window shop. That would not have happened in my day."

"Oh, Lou Lou. I'm so glad you came back," said Danielle, close to tears.

"Now, now, Danielle. Don't overwhelm her. You know Lou Lou likes her space."

"But it's just that I was so scared you wouldn't." Danielle took his hand. He hoped it wasn't too rough. Sorting the pieces of leather had been a huge job. There had been thousands. In the end he had sorted them into at least a dozen different piles, and his skin was chafed. Still, he told himself, it probably wasn't much different from Francine's, given all that she had to do at home, including handling the lye to make soap.

"But it's just that I'm still getting over Claire and Bernadette. Oh, Lou Lou. It's terrible. I've been crying for days."

They had moved into the sitting room, which was full of little sofas made of carved wood and shiny fabric. In between them were round tables with fancy legs, holding porcelain figurines of dogs and ballerinas. Lou was afraid to move in case he knocked something over.

"What happened?" asked Lou, remembering to whisper. He suddenly felt fragile, like one of the shiny glass bowls on the table at his feet.

"Claire was called back just after New Year's, Lou Lou," explained Madame Oliver. "Sister Clothilde was ill, and she wanted Claire home. You know they're very close."

"But she's coming back, right?" Lou was starting to panic. Without Claire, the team would fall apart anyway. And if it did, there was no reason for him to be here.

"No one knows, Lou Lou. And that's why it's so terrible, on top of what happened to Bernadette." Danielle was sniffling into a handkerchief.

"Bernadette?" he croaked.

"Her parents made her get engaged to some horrible man, and now she's not allowed to come back on the team. Oh, it's a disaster, Lou Lou. That's why when you didn't call I was in a complete panic. It will be hard enough to replace Claire and Bernadette, but you too ..."

"Danielle, please. Don't frighten poor Lou Lou on her first day back. Claire might still return, and there's nothing we can do about Bernadette. And you don't know if that man is horrible. Bernadette seemed happy in her letter. And of course she can't play hockey if she's married."

Madame Oliver was right. Getting married was as bad as losing a leg, for a girl.

"How's your brother, Lou Lou? Any news from him yet?" asked Madame Oliver.

Georges and his troubles suddenly seemed so far away, even though he was just up the hill at the Royal Vic.

"Lou Lou?" Danielle reached over and poked him in the arm. So he told them about Georges, giving as few details as possible. Danielle started to cry again, and Madame Oliver told him she would drive him to the hospital whenever he wanted and let him use the telephone whenever he wanted too.

That night, Lou looked across at the empty bed. He had been dreading sleeping in the same room as Claire again, listening to her beg to be allowed to roll in beside him or insist that they tell each other everything, the way she and the girls at the orphanage had. She had stopped being as pushy toward the end, but he was sure that these weeks apart would have made her just as eager again. Now he had to admit that the room was awfully quiet without her. All he could hear were the sounds of the city, things rolling and clopping and banging and people yelling in the distance.

Lou tried to picture Claire in her bed at the orphanage, just one of fifty girls all sleeping in one big room. How must she be feeling? He remembered her telling him that this was her last year of freedom before taking her vows. Was that year really going to be cut short? He knew that Claire would miss playing hockey as much as Georges did. Claire's whole face lit up on the ice. Coach Robichaud never had to urge her on. From the second her blades hit the ice on a shift, Claire was flying. No wonder! She was squeezing a whole lot of action into a short space of time.

Forty

At practise the next day Coach tried moving different people around to compensate for the loss of two top players, but nothing seemed to work. Marie-Claude tried her best on right wing, but she was no Claire. Coach tried to hide his frustration. "We still have a great team," he said. "We have Lou Lou and Danielle and our terrific goalie, Magdalène. And you McGill girls have been strong all year and you're all back. But we have to step up and play harder. Everyone will need to play their best game if we're going to win."

Maybe he was just imagining it, but Lou was sure Coach had stared longest at him as he gave his speech. It was Lou he was counting on most. In his mind, Lou saw Boss's shack at the docks, waiting for him like a peaceful hideaway. Why hadn't he just stayed there? He wasn't sure he could rescue the Bakers without Claire and Bernadette, or if he even wanted to. After all, it had been the thought of letting them — and especially Claire — down that had pushed him to return.

Their first game was against the Flyers. Lou tried to play his best, but it was like he had lead weights on his skates. Not only that, but Coach had put the two best McGill girls, Alice and Violet, on his line as wingers. Even though the word "pass" was pretty much the same in both languages, it messed Lou up to hear the girls calling out in English. He understood phrases like "I'm open" or "Give it to me" or "It's yours," but that didn't matter. He felt like he was suddenly on a different team. In the end he scored one goal, but the Bakers lost 2–1. It was the first game the Flyers had won all year.

Lou sat in his private changing room, taking longer than usual. Even though the stall door locked, he was never sure someone wouldn't jump up on the toilet next door to peek down at him. But tonight the girls were also lingering in the dressing room, deflated. Lou imagined them peeling off their clothes slowly and quietly.

He was glad Georges hadn't been able to come to this game. He wasn't steady enough on his new leg yet. Not only that, but the stump hurt from rubbing if he walked too long. But he said he'd be able to do it any day now, if he got a lift up and down the hill. Lou knew that Georges missed Audrée and wanted to get back to Saint-Christophe, but he didn't want to leave until he saw the Bakers. Lou wanted him to come to a game, but he also felt weird about his brother seeing him dressed up as a girl. No one from home had seen that yet, except for his parents the day Coach had come to the house, and that had been bad enough. He hoped Georges would be able to focus on what he did with the puck, not on what he was wearing. Still, without his usual wingers, Georges wouldn't be seeing Lou at his best.

On Sunday, no one knocked on Lou's door to ask him to join Madame Oliver and Danielle on their day of church and culture. Lou waited a while, then dressed and ran down to the docks to find Boss. He hadn't been paid yet for the leather job.

"Just in time," said Boss. "Help us bail and load the leather. Me and Jean are going selling tomorrow. Good job, by the way, young man."

Lou spent an hour tying up the piles he'd made. He had separated all the rough, suede-like pieces from the smooth leather, then sorted them by color and size: all the darks and lights together, big, small, and medium together. Every scrap had belonged somewhere. Now Lou wished he could figure out where he belonged. He and the ice were a perfect fit, he knew that, but not on this team, not anymore. But if he quit the team, going back to Saint-Christophe would be hard too. There wasn't any real hockey to play there, at least not on anything like the Victoria Rink or with a real coach. And he preferred the big city, with all its opportunities.

"Here's a buck, son. It looks like you found somewhere to stay, right?" Boss put his hand on Lou's shoulder and squeezed gently.

Lou nodded, thinking how much he'd rather be in Boss's shed than at Madame Oliver's.

"Good. Well, don't be a stranger. I might have more work. You're turning into a strong young man. Hey, Jean, look. Muscles." Boss grabbed Lou's biceps and squeezed. He was right, there was muscle there. Too bad Lou couldn't tell him why.

The next morning the phone rang at breakfast. Lou and Danielle listened to Madame Oliver saying, "I see" over and over again in French. Every now and then she threw in "That's fantastic." They held their breath as she sat down.

"Well, girls. You'll never believe it. Claire is coming back to play against the Vics on Saturday. She has permission to come back just for the weekend, for one last game. And she said she's bringing a big surprise."

Danielle shouted, "Hooray!" and jumped out of her seat. She threw her arms around Madame Oliver, almost knocking her off her chair.

"Danielle, please. A bit of control," said the older woman. But she too was smiling. She knew as well as Danielle and Lou that they didn't have a hope in hell of beating the Vics without Claire.

Georges had to see this game. Even though it would be hard for the Bakers to win without their full top lineup, Georges would at least get to see Lapensée in action. With any luck, Lou could score twice against her, like he had last time. When Lou got a chance, he asked Madame Oliver to help him call the hospital to tell him.

Forty-One

L ou and Danielle waited all day for Claire to show up. At five o'clock, Madame Oliver said they couldn't wait any longer. The game started at seven, and Coach Robichaud wanted them at the rink early to do a strenuous warm-up before facing the Vics.

The crowds were already starting to gather as usual when Lapensée was in town. Cornwall was only two hours away by train, and she'd brought half the town with her, or at least it seemed that way. They had no spectator rink of their own, so their fans had to follow them around to watch them play. Lou kept one eye on the entrance as he skated laps. Georges had said he could come tonight, and Madame Oliver had arranged for him to be picked up at the hospital. She had also put out a proper seat for him, beside the team bench. There was no way he could stand for a whole game. Now that Claire hadn't shown up, Lou wasn't as excited about Georges coming. He wouldn't be seeing the real team, the team that Lou had helped create. If Coach put the McGill girls on his wings again, he'd see Lou at his worst.

From across the ice, Lou watched Georges and Coach Robichaud shake hands. Georges's pants looked normal again, the left one hanging just like the right. But he still carried one crutch, and when he walked to the bench he had a stiff swing to his step. Only one knee could bend.

Georges and Coach talked for a long time, and Lou couldn't imagine what they were talking about: war or hockey? Coach was too old to be conscripted, but he knew his hockey. Should Lou skate over and say hello? He wanted to, but he also didn't want to. He knew Georges was going to crack up when he saw him. The sweater and tuque weren't different from what he'd wear on a boys' team. But that ballooning skirt!

"Hey, Lou Lou, come on over," Coach called out. "Say hello to your brother."

Lou skated over as slowly as he could. Georges was trying hard to hold his face straight, Lou could tell. It was like when they'd done something bad at home, and they tried to hide it from Papa over dinner. They'd be passing butter or salt and holding in their chuckles, so much so that their cheeks would be bulging. It always gave them away.

"You didn't tell me your brother was such an expert on hockey," said Coach.

"My sister doesn't like to share things, I'm sure you noticed," said Georges, winking at Lou.

"She's a quiet one all right. But we don't mind, as long as she makes noise on the ice. Especially tonight. That Lapensée is a force, I can tell you. They say they have proof she's a girl, but I still have my doubts. Still, what can I do? But Lou Lou beat her last time. She was brilliant out there."

"Yes, she told me. She also told me Lapensée was her reason for joining up."

"Really? Well, we're glad she did, whatever the reason."

Lou was content to stand and listen. He was afraid that if he opened his mouth it would be game over. He couldn't whisper in front of Georges, and his voice would boom around the rink if he yelled at Georges to quit having so much fun, the way he wanted to.

"You were in the army, Georges, so you know what I mean when I say that every team needs a leader. Lou Lou is not a talker, but she leads by example. By speed and by skill."

"You're making my sister blush, Monsieur Robichaud," said Georges.

Lou held every muscle in his face as tight as he could. What he really wanted to do was shout a string of curses at Georges. His brother was enjoying this way too much. He wished Coach would stop going on about him, making him sound so wonderful. For some reason, it only made him feel worse. Coach shouldn't be comparing him to a soldier, to someone who went out there and tried to rid the world of bad people. Lou himself was one of those bad people because of what he was doing — hiding his true self and telling the world a great big lie.

Lou had a sudden urge to rip off his uniform and reveal himself to the Coach, the way Coach wanted to reveal Lapensée. What would he have to say about Lou then?

But suddenly the ref was blowing the whistle, and Lapensée, looking bigger and meaner than ever, skated to center ice. She was glancing around, her dark eyes sharp under thick eyebrows. It was like she was trying to figure out who she was going to devour. When her eyes hit on Lou, she stopped searching. Her face broke into a wide smile, and he knew. She'd been looking for him.

Lou felt sick to his stomach as he skated over to face her for the opening drop. Then he played his worst period of the season. Every time he faced off against Lapensée he felt her breathing down on him like some steam-powered machine. Marie-Claude had been put back on right wing, and she seemed to always be a foot or two behind, which slowed Lou down. Simone, the girl who had escaped the convent, was on his left, but she wasn't much faster. The Vics' defense had fattened up over the holidays, like Lapensée. It was like they'd all eaten too much goose and tourtière or bread pudding. Because he and Claire and Bernadette had been able to pass the puck back and forth so well, he hadn't felt the impact of being pushed to the ice or rammed into the side. But now that he had to carry the puck up the middle on his own, he did. He didn't dare look right at Georges, but from the corner of his eye he caught his brother standing and shouting alongside Coach. He just prayed Georges hadn't shouted out "little brother" or "*Petit Lou.*"

He was aching when the ref blew the whistle for the first intermission. It was 3–0 for the Vics.

The girls sat with their heads down, studying their skates. Coach was talking above them. "You've got to skate faster, girls, and keep possession of the puck. Don't pass it unless you're sure you can connect. You keep turning it over to the Vics. And Danielle, I know Lapensée is big, but you're no daisy. That's why you're on defense. Stand up to her. One good shove of the hip …"

"And you could skate back with her, Marie-Claude, since you seem to like center ice. Be her shadow. Don't let her get that far into your zone with the puck. With two of you on her you'll have a better chance," said Georges.

Lou's head snapped up toward Coach. Would he like Georges stepping in and giving the team advice?

"Great idea, Georges," said Coach. "I want you to

consider yourself Lapensée's shadow from now on. You only leave her when you know you've got a clear path to the net yourself, okay?" Marie-Claude nodded. They could hear her aunt and friends blowing their horns across the rink, trying to drown out Lapensée's fans, who were shouting, "La-pen-sée, hey-hey-hey" over and over, like some bad dream.

The referee was blowing his whistle, signaling that it was time to get back to the game, when the door behind the bench swung open. Lou thought it must be some girls who'd disappeared to the washroom to fix their hair, like they usually did. But when the girls stepped closer, Lou and everyone else jumped up. It was Claire and Bernadette, all dressed in their Bakers' uniforms, their skates tied on. The entire bench screamed. The girls huddled around them, bouncing up and down. Even Lou was tempted to join in.

Claire separated herself from the circle and approached Lou. She looked different. Her hair had been cut short, and she was thinner, like she hadn't eaten enough. Her face was pale, and her eyes were a duller blue than he remembered, like they had faded. She threw her arms around him.

"Didn't think you'd ever see me again, eh, Lou?" He shook his head. "Happy?" she asked.

"Yes," he said. And it surprised him just how much it was true.

"And do you like my surprise?" she asked, pointing at Bernadette. Lou nodded. He couldn't have asked for more, especially tonight.

"How did you do it?" he asked.

"Long story. And it wasn't easy. But I can be quite persistent, you know?" He nodded again. He certainly did know. It struck him that Claire was the sort of girl who could do anything she wanted, if she set her mind to it. Except fully control her own life. He watched her scan the rink, her eyes roaming over the ice and up through the crowds. It wouldn't surprise him if she had broken through chains to get here, not that nuns were chained, but still. The water in Claire's eyes wasn't just from the cold, Lou could tell. And when she muttered, "One last time" before jumping out onto the ice, Lou knew that she meant it.

Forty-Two

B ack on the ice, Lou ignored Lapensée and focused on the puck. He glued his eyes to that black circle like it was a matter of life and death. And suddenly it was.

He could feel Claire on his right and Bernadette on his left, just like old times. They matched each other stride for stride up the ice, and when a defenseman got too close, they passed the puck across the rink. On their first shift, they were just finding each other's sticks again, but by the second their passes were closer. By the third, the puck landed on the tips of their sticks with complete precision. Their first goal was a perfect tic-tac-toe, from Bernadette to Claire to Lou. The three of them cheered and slapped each other's backs in front of the Vics' goalie. But Claire's face hadn't changed. There was still something there that bothered Lou, and something missing too, all at the same time. As he sat on the bench, he wondered what it would be like to know that this was the last time you'd be part of a team and the last time you'd hear the crowd roar and call your name. There was no doubt — it would be devastating.

The next time Lou's line was on the ice, the crowd cheered even louder. It was 3–1 for the Vics, but he could feel a goal coming. They'd never skated this fast. Claire passed him the puck, which he flicked past the defense and regained. Bernadette was speeding up the left side, banging her stick on the ice, longing for a pass. Lou hit it, and it sailed onto her stick. All she had to do was hit it past the goalie.

The crowd erupted. It was like Marie-Claude's aunt had given every single person in the crowd a horn to blow. For a split second, Lou wondered if Bernadette's future husband was in the crowd, also cheering, but it wasn't likely.

The next time out it was the same story. The three of them were flying, and their passes were so crisp and precise the Vics' defensemen could do nothing but watch the pucks float past their feet. It was like their skates were frozen inside the ice, held there in a cold grip. Bernadette carried the puck in, then let Claire take over. She skated up the right side. The defenseman stood in front of her, but Claire just swung to the side, taking the puck with her. She passed it to Lou, and he banged it home. On the other end of the ice, Magdelène made a few brilliant saves, and even Danielle was back to her old self, throwing her weight around, as if having the number one trio back on the ice gave her strength. By the end of the second period the game was tied.

The ten-minute break was torture for Lou. He just wanted to be back out there. He even forgot that Georges was sitting at the end of the bench in his army uniform, his wooden leg stretched out in front of him. He had never known such focus. It was like that night out on the lake with Georges, when nothing else had existed. Except tonight it was here, on this ice, where nothing else in the world was happening except this game that he was part of.

Coach tapped him hard on the back and said, "One more, Lou Lou. We need one more. Go out there and get it for us."

Lou looked over at Claire as they skated out for the opening faceoff. She was so beautiful in her uniform. He couldn't imagine her in the dark robes she'd wear after this. But her face hadn't changed. Their line had scored three goals, but Claire's eyes were as dull as ever. It was like she was playing by memory, but not by heart.

This was Claire's last game. Lou kept hearing those two fatal words in his head. He knew he had to do something for her. She had been the team's leader before he'd shown up, stealing that role from her. And she'd never made him feel bad about it. She'd done nothing but encourage him.

Lou skated the puck up the ice. The defenseman poked it away, sending it toward Lapensée. She flew down the ice with the speed of Newsy Lalonde. Danielle stood in front of her, puffing herself up, turning herself into a human roadblock. But Lou couldn't take any chances. He turned and headed for his own net. He caught up with Lapensée, poked his stick between her legs, and stole the puck.

Lapensée froze. He could hear her slam her stick on the ice, but he didn't care. He was closing in on the Vics' net. Claire was keeping pace on the right. He pulled back his stick, as if he was going to shoot. The Vics' goalie bounced toward him. Then he flicked the puck over to Claire. It landed on the crook of her stick. She stopped skating and shot the puck. It flew as gracefully as a bird flying off a branch.

The smile that lit her face touched Lou, right down to this toes.

The crowd chanted, *"Claire, Claire, Claire"* as she skated to the bench.

Lou didn't care who saw, not even Georges. He threw his arms around her and pulled her close.

Forty-Three

In his own private cubbyhole, Lou pulled off the Bakers' uniform. It was the last time he'd ever wear it. He'd known it the moment he passed the puck to Claire for the game-winning goal. If she had to leave, he did too. He knew that more clearly than he'd ever known anything. It just felt completely right. Maybe this was the way Georges had felt the day he and his friends had enlisted. He remembered Georges explaining it to Papa over and over again. Joining a team to become a hero had been the right thing to do. Now, leaving a team because Lou was just pretending to be a hero was also the right thing to do.

He could hear the girls through the wall. They were gathered around Claire and Bernadette, congratulating them and begging them to stay. They were the real heroes of the team, not him.

The door to the bathroom banged, and Lou knew he was no longer alone. Normally he'd be dressed by now, but he'd been lost in thought.

"Lou?" It was Claire.

"In here," called Lou, stepping into the dark skirt. Suddenly Claire's face appeared above the stall. He grabbed his sweater and held it to his flat, slightly hairy, chest.

"It's okay, Lou," Claire said, smiling down at him. "I know you're a boy. I've known it for a long time. You don't grow up in the same bedroom as fifty other girls and not learn everything about the way girls are, the way they move and talk and sleep. If you're a girl, then I'm the daughter of a king and queen."

"But you never told."

"We all have our reasons for hiding, Lou. It wasn't up to me to tell. You have to live with your lies, just like I have to live with mine." Lou let the shirt fall. Claire climbed down and knocked on the door of his stall. "Let me in."

It didn't seem right for them to be so close together, with Lou still half naked and Claire about to go off and become a nun, so Lou pulled his shirt on.

"What do you mean, Claire, about your lies? When did you lie? I mean, you're definitely not a guy." Lou was suddenly too aware that he was alone with a girl without pretending. It made everything different.

"It's what I tell people about who I am. I say my parents died, but the truth is that I had no parents. No one knows who my mother was. She left me at the convent as a baby, wrapped in a shawl. And there's even less chance I'll ever find out about my father."

"Wow," said Lou quietly.

"So you see, Lou. If I told the truth, they wouldn't want me. The only way they'd accept me is if I lied, like you had to, to get on this team."

Lou's throat tightened. "But are you sure? I mean, it wouldn't make any difference to me."

"But to your parents, or any man's parents, it would. You can't hide something like that forever."

Lou thought of the two guys at Dupuis Frères talking about Claire and how pretty she was. Would it matter to them if Claire had no parents? Or that she'd been born out of wedlock? He just didn't know. Maybe she was right. Father Béliveau certainly went on and on about how wrong it was for young people to get too close before marriage. Claire's parents had obviously done that. Would Georges want to marry Audrée if she'd been left as a baby at an orphanage?

"Don't look so sad, Lou. It's not the end of the world for me. I know what life at the convent is like, and times are changing. I want to start a girls' team back home one day. I have ideas. They just won't involve being married and having children. But not everyone who does that is happy either. You should speak to Bernadette. You know, I think I'll have more freedom than she ever will."

Lou looked into Claire's blue eyes. Scoring that winning goal had put some of the light back into them, and now they had that same glistening shine he knew so well. He threw his arms around her and pulled her close again, like he'd done on the ice. He could smell the soap she used to freshen her hair after a game, like lilacs.

"I'll never forget you, Claire," he said. "And if you ever need help with that team of yours, or anything else, you know where I live."

"Saint-Christophe. I remember." Claire leaned over and kissed Lou's cheek. He could feel himself turn hot. It wasn't really betraying Francine, being kissed by a teammate. Or kissing her back, on the cheek.

They heard the door to the bathroom open and a voice call out, "Hey, you two, ice cream for everyone. Monsieur Oliver's treat. Hurry up."

"You go first," said Lou. "I'll catch up. I have to find my brother."

"Sure, Lou," said Claire, winking. She knew he wouldn't join the team for ice cream. His plan was to rush to Madame Oliver's and grab his stuff. He'd leave a note saying his mother wanted him home, to help with Georges. She'd believe that. It was a girl's job, after all, to help others. To do what others told her to do. She'd think he was just being a dutiful daughter.

An hour later, at the shed, Boss was just leaving when Lou arrived. "You do come and go, young man. I see you have your stuff with you. Looking for a place to stay, I suppose."

"Just a few nights, Boss. I can do some cleaning in here, whatever you want."

"It's all right, son, I know I can trust you. But keep the stove going. I don't want anyone freezing to death in my shed."

Lou had bought a newspaper on the way to the port. Huddled under an old blanket that smelled of horse, the fire making odd shapes on the shed roof, Lou read the sports section and smiled. It was just as he'd hoped.

Forty-Four

"**W**here are we going, Lou?" Georges kept asking the following evening, when he and Lou were seated in the taxi.

"Stop asking. You'll see when we get there," said Lou. He wanted it to be a total surprise. He hoped he was doing the right thing. It might backfire, showing Georges the arena he might have played in one day. But he couldn't let Georges go home tomorrow without seeing the Canadiens in action. It wouldn't be fair. Papa had seen them; Lou had seen them. Now Georges had to see them too.

Lou helped Georges step down from the taxi. He watched his brother's face as it dawned on him where they were. The long roof of the Montreal Arena stretched ahead of them, and they could hear the crowd that had started to gather.

"Lou? Is this what I think it is?"

"Yes, Georges. And wait until you see our seats."

Lou had run over first thing in the morning to buy two of the best seats in the house. He'd used almost every last penny, saving enough for the taxi and a few treats, including fur rugs for them to sit on.

Georges followed Lou inside, looking around in awe as Lou had done the first time he'd seen this grand arena. And when the team started skating onto the ice to warm up, Georges's eyes grew wide as pucks. There were his heroes, skating not ten feet away. Lou watched Georges and tried to read his face. Was it just excitement, or was there also regret?

"You do amaze me, Petit Lou," Georges said finally. "You really do."

That was all Georges said for the next two and a half hours. His face was fixed on the ice as he followed the action. A few times, the players were pressed against the boards right in front of them, close enough to touch. Big Joe Malone and Didier Pitre, fighting opponents for the puck. Newsy Lalonde, Papa's favorite, with beads of sweat on his forehead, pacing behind the bench, leading his team to victory against the Ottawa Senators. Georges leaned forward when they came close, but he didn't speak, not even when someone scored. It was as if watching the Canadiens play had transported him to another world. Lou wondered if this was how it had been for his brother down in the trenches, watching but not daring to make noise.

Even during the two intermissions Georges didn't

say much. He didn't seem angry or unhappy, just intense. The silence continued all the way back up to the hospital. Lou was saying goodbye when Georges finally spoke.

"You know, Lou. You will make that team one day. I know it. You played great last night."

"Thanks, Georges." Lou gazed at his brother then suddenly reached up and hugged him. It was the first time he'd really touched Georges since his return. It felt strange, but it felt right too. It must have taken a lot for Georges to say that.

"You're welcome, Lou," said Georges.

The next day Lou surprised Georges again by showing up at the train station and announcing that he too was going home.

"But the team ..." said Georges.

"You know I didn't belong there, Georges. It wasn't going to last forever."

They watched the Gatineau hills grow larger in the distance. Saint-Christophe was nestled between them, tiny as a snowflake compared to the metropolis of Montreal. There, Georges would marry Audrée and find something to do. Lou could go back to school or find some farming work to do, and in a few years he could marry Francine. Or he could eventually go back to Montreal and work for Boss while playing hockey. The war couldn't last forever. Sooner or later there would be boys' teams again.

"You know, Lou, I've been thinking," said Georges as the train clanked over the tall steel bridge.

"What?"

"There's no reason we couldn't do it."

"Do what?"

"Start a girls' team in Saint-Christophe, or at least in the valley. There'd be plenty of girls good enough to play. We'd know how to find them better than Coach Robichaud did. Look at your girlfriend." Georges poked Lou in the ribs.

"She's not my girl—"

"Yeah, whatever. You know Francine is every bit as good as Claire. I mean, she's just as fast. With time she'd puck-handle the same way too."

"But Father Béliveau ..."

"Father Béliveau doesn't get to decide everything, Lou. Times are changing. If we want to start a girls' team, he can't stop us. There were women working with us overseas, and believe me, they were no fragile daisies."

Claire had said the same thing — times were changing. The world was changing, and that was why people everywhere were fighting. Georges was right. Father Béliveau didn't really have the authority to stop them.

Lou looked out the window and thought about it. He liked the idea, but he needed to know that Georges would take the game just as seriously with girls playing. After all, Lou wouldn't have taken the idea of a girls' team seriously two months ago. But now he thought about Bernadette, Danielle, Marie-Claude, Magdalène, and, especially, Claire. To them, the team was serious. It wasn't something they were just playing around with until they could do the real thing. For those girls, it might be the most real thing they were ever going to do.

"Georges," Lou said, "if we're going to form a team, we have to do it and mean it. The girls who play on those teams have big dreams too, just like we do."

"Okay, Lou, but you know it's different. They can't make hockey a career, like we can."

"Why not? We can help change that."

"That's crazy, Lou. Would you want Francine playing hockey if you were married and let's say you had kids? It's just not practical. It wouldn't happen."

"But you said the world is changing, right? I mean, isn't that why you went overseas, to help make it better?"

Georges turned and didn't answer. Now, he stared out the window. They were passing towns that resembled their own, with the frozen lake shining through the trees, the white-steepled church, the clapboard houses with smoke spewing from chimneys, stacks of wood piled beside porches.

"Okay, little brother," he said finally, turning back to Lou. "You win. You know, you do amaze me, Petit Lou. You really do." Then he turned back to the window, deep in thought. Lou wondered where he was. Was he back overseas, in Belgium? Or was he at an arena, in charge of a bench of girls?

Lou saw Claire, speeding down the ice, her blond hair horizontal behind her. She didn't clomp as she skated, like some people did. She slid gracefully, with long strides. That was how she would teach the orphans on her team to skate. And when they scored, they'd throw their arms up in the air, raising their sticks high, just like she did. If he and Georges did start a team, maybe he and Claire would meet again one day, at a rink, her team against his. And if girls' hockey lasted a long time, after the war was over, maybe Georges and Audrée's daughters would play against Claire's orphans. Maybe his and Francine's daughters, too. But that was thinking way too far ahead.

Suddenly, Lou bolted upright. "But, Georges," he said. "There's only one hitch."

"What?"

"What'll we do when we play the Bakers?"

Georges laughed. "That's easy. We'll dress you up as a girl and sit you behind the bench with a horn."

"Ha ha," responded Lou.

Maman and Papa and Audrée were like tiny puppets in the distance, but they were already waving. Lou and Georges looked at each other and smiled. Lou felt his brother's presence beside him, just as he always had. The wooden leg stretched out under the chair ahead, but he was still the same older brother. Lou thought how they were a small family, the smallest in Saint-Christophe. But they had always had big dreams.

Acknowledgements

Thank you to the CBC for producing the series *Hockey: A People's History*. Episode 3 ("Empires on Ice") provided the spark for this book in the form of Ada Lalonde, a seventeen-year-old player discovered by the coach of the Montreal Westerns in rural Quebec. Ada was supposed to rival Albertine Lapensée and Eva Ault, but turned out not to be the right fit for the team. She did, however, set my imagination flying. I'd also like to thank the generous financial support of the Conseil des arts et des lettres du Québec. Thanks also to the town of Taos, New Mexico, for being so artistically inspirational and scenically beautiful; it was there that the bulk of the book was written. Finally, thanks once again to my family who always encourage me to lace up my metaphorical skates and get out there on the ice and write, even on days when the ice seems thin. I couldn't do it without you.